Secrets of
Sleeping Indian
Mountain

Jana Nolan

Secrets of Sleeping Indian Mountain

Jana Nolan

Earth Star Publications
www.earthstarpublications.com

FIRST EDITION
First Printing October 2015

ISBN 978-0-944851-43-2

Printed in the United States of America

INTRODUCTION

For those of you who haven't read any of my books, I can only say that this book has been a tremendous joy and challenge for me to write. To explain why I chose the title is only to say that it was inspired by this area where I have chosen to live.

Living below Sleeping Indian Mountain has been an experience in itself. The mountain alone is very unique. Many stories come to mind from townspeople who have lived in the area their entire lives. Because of all the tales of the mountain that have been told to me, I took their stories and turned them into this creative, fictional story that will thrill you and chill you.

I am a country girl who has spent many years enjoying the beauty of the outdoors. Born and raised in Montrose, Colorado, I spent years gaining the knowledge it took to give to you a book that pretty much says it all.

The cover doesn't do the beauty of the mountain the justice it deserves, but with what you see, I am taking you into a new direction which will keep you guessing until the end.

Sit back and be prepared for the horrific stories that you are about to read.

Someone once said to me, and I would like to share it with you, "Sometimes reality is fiction." The reality of many things is fiction to others.

My stories that I tell in this book are meant to give you a perspective of reality with much intent of being fiction. After reading the tales and secrets of Sleeping Indian Mountain, only *you* can decide what you choose to believe. Just remember that again, sometimes reality is fiction. But then again, is it?

The mountain has many secrets that have been told by the people of the small town below the mountain. For several years, some of the townspeople chose to ignore them, not because of disbelief, but because of fear.

As for me, I choose to live below it. In the still of the night, I sit and listen to many sounds that echo off the mountainside.

Fact or fiction is why the people of the town believe only what they choose to believe, and hear.

Let your mind wander as you dwell into the

past and present stories of the living and the dead.

Each day, listen to the wind, as it will talk to you. Even in the quietest moments you will hear someone, or some *thing,* telling you what you need to know.

The Secrets of Sleeping Indian Mountain will take you to a place that you have never been.

As you read, listen to what surrounds you. Don't be afraid ... or should you?

CONTENTS

PART 1

PART 2

PART 3

PART ONE

1

My Best Surprise

Some people look at crying as a sign of weakness. As for myself, I feel as if it is the cleansing of one's soul. Whether it be happy tears, or sad tears.

Then again, there are a lot of things that I believe that some people have either made fun of, or out of fear of not wanting to know, find out about or out of disbelief, refuse to accept.

This is where my story starts. Only you can choose to believe what you want to.

My name is Malon Moore. My friends call me Mylo for short. As I was growing up, some of the kids in school would scarf at my name. Their favorite dig at me was, "Did your parents think you were a boy when you were born?" My reply back was, "Maybe?"

This was only the beginning of my learning that people can be cruel. Whether they are a kid or an adult. The truth being said, I chose the name myself.

I was born and raised in a small town in Colorado. I grew up loving the outdoors and the mountains. Truly a country girl by heart. Everyone around the entire area knew each other.

When a neighbor needed help, everyone that could help pitched in. The town that I am referring to is Applegrove. It's located at the bottom of Sleeping Indian Mountain.

Many stories circulated around the town for many years. The people of Applegrove called them strange and bizarre happenings that were believed to have occurred on the mountain or about the mountain itself.

Mainly, the older people in my small town are the ones who lived, or relived, the different events that haunted them for years. For some, many more years to come.

In order to tell you my story, I need to go back in time. My earliest memory starts at the age of 5. As far as I remember, at that age the only thing that stands out in my mind was the day that my father and mother brought home the best surprise that any kid could receive. They brought me a horse.

I chose the name "Rocky" for him as he had a hump on his back that felt like a rock when I rode him bareback without a saddle.

Rocky was red in color, with a long mane. He stood tall and proud. When he saw me running in the pasture to greet him, he put his head down to nudge me. He liked me as much as I did him.

My father would ride with me on Rocky until he was sure in his mind that I would be safe. It wasn't long before I had learned everything I needed to know. By the time I turned 6, Father was ready to let me ride by myself.

On my sixth birthday, Mother had dressed me in a yellow dress with a black sash. She had invited neighbors and family to the house to celebrate my birthday.

There was one guest missing. This would be my best friend, Rocky. Mother told me that after the opening of the presents, cake and ice cream, I could change into my jeans, shirt and boots. Rocky could join me and the party.

This was the beginning of a long friendship which led to many years filled with adventure that we both shared together.

I know that living below Sleeping Indian Mountain was a dream that a lot of kids my age wished they could have had. That was where Rocky and I chose to explore.

Mother and Father extended limitations where we could go on the mountain. When the sun started to go down, I was expected to be back in the yard, with Rocky in the pasture to graze.

Every day when the bridle came off, I would pat Rocky on his head, followed by a soft kiss.

When I ran off the school bus on school days, I rushed to my bedroom to change clothes. Out the back door, I ran to find Rocky either in the pasture or in the barn.

Many nights before it was completely dark, I would stand at my bedroom window, or sit on my bed, and plan another adventure for us to discover the next day.

Days, months and years passed. I had gone from

age 6 to 16. I could tell that Rocky was struggling some days to interact with our journeys. He was moving slower. Our trips exploring the lower part of Sleeping Indian were filled with more rules set by Mother and Father.

There were many days when there were too many clouds, and too much fog, to even be allowed to leave the yard. The weather in Applegrove was worse than it had ever been before.

When morning came, I picked up my school books and was ready to walk out onto the back porch when I was met by my father and mother coming toward me through the screen door.

The look on my father's and mother's faces was very sad, and somewhat distant. When Father looked at me, several tears dropped from his eyes. Knowing how much Rocky meant to me, it was hard for him to deliver the news to me about Rocky.

With tears still streaming from his eyes, Father said, "Mylo, I have bad news to tell you. Last night your mother and I heard a disturbing sound outside. Getting up out of bed, I grabbed my rifle. As I rubbed my eyes, trying to wake up, I told your mother to wait for me in the house, and not to go outside looking for me. When I went out the back door, I walked to the barn to check on Rocky. He wasn't there.

"I then changed my direction and checked the pasture. There, lying on the ground next to the drain ditch, was Rocky. It looked like he had stepped into a hole and fell. Since I had been gone longer than your mother thought I should have, she loaded her rifle and came to find me. What killed Rocky was an animal of some sort. We believe it went back to Sleeping Indian."

All I could do was cry and say, "It's not fair. Why Rocky? *Why?*"

"I know, Mylo, that Rocky meant a lot to you. Maybe a bear killed him. She might have thought that he was a threat to her cubs."

I was only 16, but even *I* knew that Father would know the sound of a bear, and not just a disturbing sound. At that time I thought that Father had told me everything.

Mother put her arms around me and said, "Remember, Mylo, it's okay to cry." Those words stayed with me my whole life. She, too, was crying and rubbing her eyes, trying not to.

Every day after that just wasn't the same without Rocky in my life.

On graduation night, dressed in my cap and gown, I went to my bedroom window and opened the curtain. As I looked outside, I said out loud, "Rocky, you are out there somewhere. I wish you were here with me tonight, so I could ride you to the high school. You would be there to watch me graduate. Remember when I was 6, and you came to my birthday party?" Several tears dropped from my eyes and fell to the floor as I talked to my best friend.

I closed the curtain, walked to my bedroom door, and turned off the light switch. That night was a new beginning of a new chapter in my life. Other journeys were waiting for me, so this was my way of letting go of my past, and telling myself that I accepted my future.

2

Adventure Waiting to Happen

After high school graduation, I stayed around Applegrove for a few years and helped my father with the ranch. I also worked at a small store in town as a clerk for a few days a week.

The store has a small area in the middle of it, where customers can sit, talk and rest. Mainly, the older people of the town sit there. As my grandmother would say, "They go there to chew the fat." For those of you who are clueless about what this means, it is talking about anything , and everything that comes to mind in a conversation.

The same people congregate in the store to tell stories of either their past or present occurrences that have or had taken place recently or in the past.

It being a small store, there is no way that anyone can avoid hearing their conversations. Believe me, I tried. Some things they discussed were way more than what I wanted to hear.

After all, I grew up in this area and wanted to believe that it was just a calm and uneventful town. How little did I know at that time, it was anything but.

The conversations seemed to always lead to different secrets of Sleeping Indian Mountain.

For years, Rocky and I had spent every day exploring as much of that mountain as we could. There were times that I felt like Rocky and I were being watched, but I just attributed it to maybe the wind that blew up there, or my wild imagination.

That day, as I stood there, I was amazed at what I was hearing. For me, knowing these people my entire life, it was hard for me to believe that they were making this stuff up.

It was my last day working at the old country store. Tomorrow I would be on my way to a new journey in my life. My new direction was New York City.

No doubt that every young girl or boy, at one time in their lives or another, has wondered how the other half live, if they were born and raised in the country.

After hearing stories of the mountain that I loved that day, and being adventurous, in my mind I knew that when I returned to Applegrove, there would be more exploring because of the strange and bizarre stories I was hearing, that Sleeping Indian Mountain possessed for many years.

These secrets would still be here, even if some of the townspeople who experienced them weren't. As strange as the stories were, or sounded, there were many reasons why, when I was growing up, I had to be in the house before it got dark.

After I started driving, no one was allowed to drive up the mountain road when the county had the road blocked and the barriers were in place.

It being time for me to leave the store and return home, I had plans to just spend every moment with my parents. I walked over to the owner of the store to hug her and thank her. Because of her giving me this job, it would pay for my journey to the city that never sleeps, that I had read about in books.

"Megan, thank you for hiring me. I will send you a postcard."

Megan hugged me back, saying, "Mylo, you have been a real joy to work with. When you come back home, I would love to have you work for me again."

"Thank you, Megan. I *will* be returning home, but I am not sure when."

"The best of luck to you."

I then left the store, and on my way home all the stories kept going through my mind. Especially the story that Ralph Winters told about the unexplainable sounds, such as the ones that my parents had heard years ago when Rocky was killed. Ralph and his family had heard these sounds close to their home.

As Ralph Winters put it, "It wasn't a dog! This came from a large animal of some sort. Years ago, Old Jake Peters and I decided to go fishing up on the mountain. When we were getting our fishing poles out of my Jeep, we heard howling, or some horrible sound like rustling of the bushes. I wanted to stay, but Old Jake got scared and put his pole back in the

Jeep and said, 'Ralph, we are going home. I didn't come all this way up here today for this!' "

As Ralph sat at that table in the store, he was, of course, poking fun at Jake for wanting to leave that day without even getting his fishing line wet.

Then Bob Porter asked Ralph, "Weren't you just a little bit afraid as well, Ralph?"

"Okay, yes. It did frighten me as well, but I had my rifle with me," Ralph replied.

With Bob laughing, he said, "What were you going to do, Ralph, shoot the bush that was rustling, making some weird sound?"

"Go ahead and poke fun at me, Bob, if you want. But you weren't there that day to hear it. Pay attention to some of the other stories, and you will see why some of us here are frightened. Maybe you haven't experienced anything yet, but don't scarf at us that have."

Of course Bob was speechless, as he and his family didn't live as close to Sleeping Indian Mountain as some of the rest of us did. He told Ralph that he was sorry for disbelieving him.

I was pretty sure at that time that the reason Bob acted the way he did that day was because of either the fear of the unknown, or that because this hadn't happened to him. It was easier for him to ignore it and pretend as if something like that didn't exist. In the store that day, after I left, there was another story told by Ralph Winters that I didn't hear, but would hear before long.

I had reached my home and was ready to spend

what time I had left in the day talking to Mother and Father. It was starting to rain and was getting dark. An adventure was waiting for me at daylight.

I parked my car in the garage and walked outside of it to enter the door of the back porch. Then, I turned around and looked out at the pasture, where my best friend had his own private grave. I sure did miss him.

The morning that Father and Mother had heard unusual sounds—the night Rocky died—was something that I tried not to think about. If I did, that would mean that once again, every time when I turned off my bedroom light switch, I would be saying goodbye to Rocky in my way.

Now, many years later, going to New York, I knew that my destiny would not be living out my life in a city. There would be a time when I would be coming home again to explore Sleeping Indian Mountain, to see what all the stories were about.

3

Next Journey

Morning came too soon for me. My mind wouldn't allow me to sleep. All I did was think about the different stories I had overheard at the country store yesterday.

I always wondered why Mother, as I was growing up, would hold my hand and keep me away from where all the stories were being passed around among everyone sitting at that table. At the time, she believed that I was too young to hear them, and I might hear something that could frighten me.

Well, she was right as I am grown up now and frightened about what is waiting for me to discover on the mountain when I return home.

I was ready for my day of driving to begin. Mom had cooked a huge breakfast and packed food and drink in a cooler for my journey. I was sure that there was much more than I could eat in three or four days of traveling.

My excitement of going to a big city and knowing that Mother and Father were excited for me, but sad as well, brought forth many emotions that day. They were nervous and worried as the only thing I knew, and had ever known, was country living surrounded by small towns.

After the prayer, as we ate, I had questions for my father.

"Father, this might not be the right time to bring this up, but to be honest, I don't know of a good time."

Father looked over his glasses at me and asked, "What is it, Mylo? I am open to talk about anything you want to know about or talk about."

"For some time now, I couldn't help hearing stories about Sleeping Indian Mountain in the old country store. I tried not to listen, but yesterday the men at the table were talking so loud, I couldn't keep from hearing them and everything that they said. I have wondered about so many things growing up, and now I am old enough to know the truth. I just need you to confirm that all the stories being told are true and real."

As my dad was eating, he was listening to my words. He stopped eating and wiped his chin with his napkin to reply to me.

"Mylo, you know that neither your mother nor myself have ever misled you about anything. Yes, when you were growing up, we didn't tell you probably everything that we should have, but we didn't want you growing up in a world of fear and doubt. I know what you want to know about now, and yes, it's time to tell you what I know. Are you wanting to know about the secrets of Sleeping Indian Mountain?"

"Yes, Father, I am."

"There are many stories that our townspeople have told for many years," Father said as he took a sip of coffee.

I replied, "Yes, it is a beautiful mountain that all of us live below. The stories that are circulating are strange, bizarre and scary. I am wondering why you and mother allowed me for many years—knowing what people were saying—to ride Rocky up on the mountain and explore the area."

"Mylo, I knew that what was told of the mountain was something at least to others in our town. There hasn't been any real proof established yet, showing anything. I also knew that you would be safe. You see, Mylo, there was no way that even in in a day of riding up that mountain road, you and Rocky would have been able to ride to the top of the mountain. Mother and I did give you boundaries of how far up you could ride. After Rocky was killed, if you remember, I became more protective and the rules around here got stronger.

"Whatever this is that's happening on the mountain, it started coming down into the valley at times, and all the stories of the people that say they had an experience from it became more frequent. When you got your car, you were not allowed on the mountain at all. The last time has been many years ago, when you turned 16, and Rocky got killed. That morning is when your mother and I told you to stay off of the mountain altogether."

"I do remember, Father. I wasn't sure why, but do remember how sad I was when Bill Baker's father went up on the mountain and found Bill dangling from a tree. Some of us were in shock for days. He was the captain of our football team, who had scholarships waiting for him. The sheriff said Bill had killed himself, but now—like all the stories I have heard—there is no doubt in my mind that someone, or some *thing,* took Bill's life."

Dad and I agreed that we had talked enough about this for now. I had a long drive ahead of me. We would discuss it more in depth when I returned.

We finished breakfast and, with tears, hugs and goodbyes, I was ready for a journey that, at the time of leaving, I had no idea would lead me back here to pursue the secrets of the mountain that I loved.

After I backed out of the garage, I turned around to wave one last time to my parents. The radio was on and turned up. Time to drive away.

4

Magic of the Park Bench

New York City, as I had read about, was filled with hundreds of people walking and driving everywhere. There were sirens sounding every hour of the day. City life was so much different than the country life that I had grown up with.

My intentions were not just to visit the city, but to also find a job for a year or so. I wanted to make some money and go back home. There I would buy a ranch of my own.

I had bought a newspaper and had circled many job opportunities. With sore feet and uncomfortable shoes, I continued my search in hopes of finding employment.

Hours had gone by and it was time to take a short break. I found a food vendor who was selling hotdogs. I bought one and walked over to a park bench to rest and eat the hotdog.

As I sat there, a man who looked to be about eight years older than I was walked up to me and asked, "Do you mind if I sit down on this bench?"

"No," I replied. "I don't mind at all."

As we ate together, both of us were exchanging

glances back and forth. In fact, I was very happy to have the company with him sitting there.

I grew up being told that a person's eyes reveal a lot about the person. This man's soft brown eyes were beautiful. Instead of waiting for him to say something else, I blurted out, "My name is Malon Moore. Better known as Mylo to my friends."

The man took his napkin, like my father did, and wiped his chin and mouth. He then said, "Mylo— that is a cute nickname. I am very happy to meet you. I could be wrong, but seeing a newspaper beside you, I am assuming that you are looking for a job. My name is Adam Belmar. If you don't mind, I would like to tell you that you are very attractive."

Adam reached his hand out to shake mine. What he said blew my mind. I hadn't been in New York City a week, and already I felt as if I had found a new friend.

"You are right, Adam. Yes, I need a job. Also, thank you for the compliment."

"If you aren't busy this evening, Malon, I would love to take you to a nice restaurant for dinner."

There was a part of me at that moment that felt hesitant, but the other part of me responded. "Yes, Adam, I would love to have dinner with you tonight."

After agreeing that we would meet at a restaurant called Stamo's, it was time to leave the bench and resume my job hunt.

"Thank you, Malon, for accepting my invitation. I will meet you inside the lobby at 7:00."

"Thank you for asking, Adam. I will be on time."

After exchanging again another smile to each other, we walked away in different directions.

At 7:00 I arrived at Stamo's only to see Adam standing outside, talking to an older man in what appeared to be an expensive suit. I could see that this man had money to burn.

Not knowing whether I should interrupt the conversation to approach Adam, I stood there waiting to see if he noticed me. Both men were in deep discussion about something. I could barely hear some of the conversation, and was very much intrigued by it.

They seemed to be talking about a project that had been going on for many years. For some reason, Adam's smile disappeared. At that moment, I felt like maybe I should leave, when Adam saw me standing there and motioned for me to come over to him.

When I approached them, Adam smiled and said, "Malon, I am so sorry to keep you waiting. I would like to introduce you to my father. Malon Moore, this is Terry Belmar. He is the owner of Wayne Belmar Research Industries. The company was founded by my grandfather many years ago."

"I am very pleased to meet you, Mr. Belmar," I replied.

"Thank you, Malon. It is *Doctor* Belmar, as I am a scientist, but Mr. Belmar works too. Adam told me that he had met a very attractive young lady today, and was bringing her here for a lovely dinner. I had a dinner meeting with some of the company directors and ran into Adam as I was leaving.

"He also told me that you are looking for employment here in our fair city. It just so happens that I have some openings that are available. If you are interested, stop by tomorrow morning. The lady you will need to speak with is Doctor Ann Neil."

"Thank you, Doctor Belmar. It was a pleasure meeting you, and very nice of Adam to mention to you that I needed to find a job here. I will be there tomorrow morning. Thank you again."

"Adam, I will leave you and Malon now. We will discuss what we were talking about at a later date. Malon, Adam, I bid you both a good night."

I watched for a brief moment as Doctor Belmar walked away. There was something about this man that intrigued me. At that moment, I didn't know that over the course of time, it would give me the answer why.

I then felt Adam's hand softly touch my arm as he said, "Malon, are you okay?"

"Yes, Adam. I am sorry I drifted off for a while. Your father seems very nice, but for some unknown reason, I feel like I have seen him before. Thank you for telling him that I was looking for work."

"You're welcome, Malon. My father and I don't see eye-to-eye at times, but we do on the fact that you are a very attractive young lady. Now, let's go in as we have a table waiting for us."

5

Employment and Anticipation

As we sat at the table and as I looked around the room, I felt very comfortable being there with him. It looked to me as if Adam's family had money, but it also looked like he was the kind of man that had riches but didn't make it his life's ambition, as he wanted to just enjoy life and the meaning of it.

After dinner, we took a carriage ride through Central Park. We talked and laughed for hours. When the excitement of the evening was over and Adam had accompanied me safely to my hotel room door, he said, "Malon, I, too, work for my father. I also am a scientist. I would love it if we could talk some more after your interview with Ann Neil in the morning."

"That would be great. Thank you again for the evening. I will never forget it. See you in the morning."

Adam took my hands and softly squeezed them. He smiled at me one last time before he walked away.

After I unlocked my hotel door and entered, closing it behind me, I turned on the light and stood against the door, and smiled again.

Something inside of me felt like I had known Adam for many years. It was time for me to come back down from my fantasy of the evening and prepare myself for tomorrow. Not knowing if I would get the job at Wayne Belmar Industries, I still needed to focus on that first, and then maybe on Adam later. My day was done.

When my alarm sounded the next morning, I turned it off and covered my head with the pillow. This was something I had done for many years. In my mind I could hear Mother saying, "Don't go back to sleep, Mylo. It is time to rise and shine."

So I took the pillow down and climbed out of bed. This was going to be a great day for me. At least, I was making it that way.

Later, after stopping for coffee, I was driving through the city and could see a towering, huge building with the words WAYNE BELMAR RESEARCH INDUSTRIES on it. It also had underground parking where I could park my car. When I left my car, it took me several steps before I reached an elevator that took me to the first floor, the lobby.

When the elevator door opened, I saw many people standing and walking, wearing white research jackets. Others that worked there were in suits or nice dresses. It appeared to be definitely business-like.

As I walked into the room from the outdoor elevator, I saw an older woman sitting at a desk. I walked over to her. "Hello, I have an appointment with a doctor today for an interview. Her name is

Ann Neil. Will you please direct me to her office?" I asked.

"Yes, you must be Malon. Doctor Belmar told me that you would be here today to speak with Doctor Neil about employment."

"I am, and I'm very excited about the probability of maybe working for this company."

"Okay, Malon, so happy you are here as Doctor Neil is expecting you. Her office is on the eighth floor. I will point you in the direction you need to go. Follow the signs to the elevator. There will be a big sign on the wall, letting you know the office number on the door. Good luck!"

I thanked her as she pointed in the direction of how to find the elevator. When I entered, I pushed the button for the eighth floor. I was amazed as even the largest hospital in the surrounding areas of my home town didn't have eight floors. With this building, there were twelve long and huge floors.

When the elevator came to a stop and the door opened, I could see a big sign on the wall that had the name ANN C. NEIL printed on it. Also the office number, 812, with arrows showing me the numbers and directions of when to turn and go down a new hallway. I finally found it. Once again, there was a lady with glasses on that had slipped part way down her nose, sitting at her desk, typing. She stopped and asked, "Can I help you?"

"Yes, my name is Malon Moore. I have an interview with Doctor Ann Neil today."

"Yes, Miss Moore. Doctor Neil is expecting you."

After picking up her phone and announcing that I was there, she told me I could go into Doctor Neil's office. I thanked her and, feeling somewhat nervous but excited, I opened Doctor Neil's office door. Sitting at the desk was a beautiful blond woman who was also wearing a white research jacket.

As she stood up, she extended her hand to shake mine. Then, as she sat down, she said, "Your name, Malon, is very pretty. I lived in Italy for years and always loved that name. I understand that you are interested in working here. I need you to fill out these papers, sign them, and then I will review them as I interview you."

"Thank you," I said as I took the papers from her hand.

As I was writing, Doctor Neil received a phone call. She excused herself and took the phone to a connecting room.

I continued to write as I completed the application. There were many questions on it that I had never encountered before on any job application.

Knowing that I was getting interviewed for a position here at one of the biggest companies in New York City, but not knowing exactly what my job would be here, I wanted to make this interview the best one that I had ever had.

When I was almost finished, I heard from the connecting room, where Doctor Neil was still on the phone, that her voice appeared raised. I heard the words, "I *know,* Terry, but I—like you—didn't expect things in that area to get out of control. You are the only one that should know how to stop this. Malon is here now, and I am about to interview her. We can talk more about this matter later." She ended the call and entered the office.

Sitting at her desk, I couldn't help but notice that whatever the conversation was with Doctor Belmar, as I suspected, had made her feel very uncomfortable.

I finished the application and handed it to her. As Doctor Neil reviewed it, she asked, "Malon, you come from the town of Applegrove, Colorado?"

"Yes, I do. I grew up there."

Doctor Neil didn't say a word, but her voice sounded strained when she then said, "I know exactly where that town is."

This surprised me as Applegrove was so small, I couldn't even find my home town on a road map.

She continued to review my application, and then she said, "I can see that you can type, file and take shorthand."

"Yes," I replied.

She continued to read about practically my whole life history as I sat there, rubbing and clinching my hands together. By then, I was more nervous and afraid that I wasn't going to pass her test.

Then she looked at me and said, "Malon, you have quite a résumé. The application looks great. Even though you have no experience with office work, I am going to give you the job. You will be working with Doctor Shawn Phillips, handling different paper work that is assigned to you on a daily basis. From what I can see, you should be an asset to Wayne Belmar Research Industries."

At that moment, I didn't know whether to laugh or cry. I knew I needed a job, but didn't think I would qualify for one this good. I shook her hand and thanked her for giving me the chance.

Before I left the office, she said, "Stop at my assistant's desk and complete the rest of the paper work before you leave."

I told her I would. This job was much more than I expected for a first job in New York City. I completed what I needed to at her office assistant's desk. I was ready to move on to phase two of my day. That would be going to tell Adam the good news.

6

Beginning of a Bigger Adventure

Across from Doctor Neil's office door, outside her office, was another sign with Adam's name on it. Feeling very excited about my new job, I couldn't wait to share the news with him.

I took the elevator to the top floor, where his office was. When I entered, I saw Adam standing at his office assistant's desk, talking to her and handing her some papers. Adam looked so handsome in his white lab jacket.

He looked up and said, "Malon, so happy to see you."

"You too, Adam."

"Please come into my office."

As I walked toward him, I noticed the office assistant staring at me. Maybe she thought that I was there to replace her in the office, or she was probably just wondering why I was there.

When Adam and I were in his office, he closed the door and asked, "Did Ann Neil hire you?"

Still excited over getting the job, I said, "Yes, she did, and I am very grateful to you for mentioning to your father that I needed employment. I am grateful that Doctor Neil is giving me the opportunity to work here and prove myself. I was hired as an office assistant."

"You will do fine, Malon. I would like to talk to you today as we have lunch. I'm sure you have questions about your job and what the research is all about here. Do you like Chinese food?"

"Yes, I do like Chinese food, and yes again, on questions."

We sat down on a couch in his office. Adam said, "Good, then I will ask Diane to order it for us. We can talk as we are waiting for the food."

Instead of calling her desk, he walked to the door and told her to order in. Also, that he didn't want to be disturbed after the food arrived.

He shut the door and came back to sit beside me. Then he looked into my eyes and said, "I was going to make reservations for us at an expensive restaurant today, Malon, for lunch. But instead, I would love to do that for this evening. Will you join me for drinks, dinner and dancing later?"

"I would love to, Adam. Having lunch here will give me the opportunity to ask you some questions that I do have on my mind."

"Okay, shoot, Malon. What do you want to know?"

"The interview with Doctor Neil went well. Tomorrow I will find out more, but today I would like to hear about Wayne Belmar Research Industries, and what is being researched here."

"As I told you last night, my grandfather founded

this company many years ago. There are many research projects that are done here. Anywhere from lab rats, monkey, DNA, and much more. Some of them—I, too, have been involved with—and others my father has excluded me from. Those projects he has included Ann Neil and Shawn Phillips to help him in his research. They are both his right hand most of the time. They all work well together, and have for many years."

"All of this sounds very interesting. I can't wait to get started."

There was a soft knock on the office door. Diane, the office worker, came in. She handed Adam the bag of food.

Adam reminded her that he didn't want to be disturbed, and to hold any calls that might come in. Also, he told her that when she finished her work, she could go home for the day.

After the office door shut, Adam and I exchanged smiles as we sat on his couch, talking about whatever came to mind in conversation. We ate and agreed on a time for the restaurant. I had been there for hours, and it was time for me to leave.

When I was walking away from Adam's office door, I saw Doctor Belmar talking to Doctor Neil in the hallway. I excused myself as I passed them, walking to the elevator. As I rounded the corner of the hall and stood waiting for the elevator to reach the twelfth floor, I overheard Doctor Neil and Doctor Belmar talking.

"I hired Malon today, Terry, as an office worker.

She, I believe, will be an asset here, but there is one thing about her that concerns me. She is from Applegrove, Colorado. You need to be careful with what you tell Adam. Keep an eye on her, if you need to."

"What! I can't believe it!" Doctor Belmar replied.

By then, my elevator door opened, and as I entered the elevator, I left there, wondering how the small town that I came from was so important in a conversation and up for discussion with my work here that I would be doing. It shouldn't matter where I had lived before moving to the city. All that either one of them should be thinking about was whether or not I could do my job properly. Why did Doctor Belmar say, "What? I can't believe it"?

When I left the building to go back to the hotel, I felt uncomfortable. The excitement of working for Wayne Belmar Research Industries was starting to fade. I needed a pick-me-up, which was always my father. He always had a way of making me feel better about anything on any subject that I talked to him about.

As soon as I closed the door to my hotel room, I walked over to the phone to call home. The first one to answer was Mother.

"Mother, it's Mylo."

"Mylo, how are you, dear?"

"I'm good, and thought I would give you and Father a call, so I can let both of you know what's new in my life."

"So happy you called. I will put it on speaker phone. Then you can talk to both of us at the same time."

"Okay, Mother."

"Mylo, it's your father."

"Hello, Father. It's so good to talk to you and Mother again. A lot has happened since we last spoke."

"Good or bad, Mylo? Are you all right in the city?"

"Everything is fine here, and happening much faster in my life than I expected it to. A couple of days ago, I met a very nice man named Adam, in the park, while sitting on a bench eating a hotdog. He saw my newspaper as I was looking for a job. Before we left there, Adam asked me out to dinner. I accepted his invitation. That evening, outside the restaurant where we were to meet, I met his father, who offered me an interview with a company that he inherited from his father. I went to this huge building today. After meeting with this lady that interviewed me, she gave me a chance to work there as an office assistant."

"That's great, Mylo!" Father replied.

"Yes, it is, but when the lady read my résumé, she saw that I was from Applegrove, Colorado, and her facial expression changed. Then, when I left her office, I went to tell Adam that I had gotten the job. When I left his office on my way to the elevator, I saw the lady who is a scientist—just like Adam and his dad. She was standing in the hall, talking to

Adam's father about me. She told him that I came from Applegrove, Colorado, and that she had hired me. She told him to be careful and if Adam knew anything. His response was very strange as he told her that he couldn't believe it. Because of this, Father, my excitement is changing, and I am wondering why the town of Applegrove is a big deal."

"Mylo, who are you working for?" Father asked.

"Wayne Belmar Research Industries, Father. Adam Belmar was his grandson. Doctor Terry Belmar was his son that became the owner when Doctor Wayne Belmar passed away."

"I don't believe I have heard of this company, but many years ago, there was a research company that came to town. They were in the area for a while, and as far as I know, they haven't been back. We all got told that they were doing research on some sort of project on Sleeping Indian Mountain. You were very young at that time. You and Rocky were also spending time on the mountain, exploring it.

"The two men that came here seemed very nice and looked harmless, so your mother and I didn't worry about you. Who knows? This could be the same research company. I have no idea, but I do know that the rest of the townspeople didn't complain about them."

"Okay, maybe that is why Doctor Belmar and the other doctor that hired me reacted the way they did. Doctor Belmar did work closely with his father before he passed away."

"Could be, Mylo. The new job does sound

interesting, and I know you will do very well at it. Now tell me about this young man named Adam."

"Adam, like I said, is a scientist that does different experiments and projects for his father, as the other scientists that work there do. He has been very respectful toward me. Right now, he is the only friend I have in the city. Oh, yes, he is very handsome." I had to giggle a little when I told Father the last part of the information he was looking for.

"Mylo, it sounds like you are about to endeavor in a bigger adventure than you and Rocky ever shared. Enjoy your new job, but in the same token, be careful at it. Take it slow with Adam, and remember that your mother and I are always here for you."

"I know you both are. I will be careful with everything. Thank you, and I will talk to you both soon," I replied.

Once again, my father had helped me. The excitement was back on with my new job and with Adam.

I had to get ready for my dinner date.

The only thing I didn't know about at that time was the conversation between my parents after our conversation ended. There would come a day when I would find out what they said to each other at a different date and time.

7

Strange Conversation

The evening with Adam was again fun and meaningful. The restaurant was elegant and expensive. We dined and danced for hours. This time, at my hotel door, Adam gave me a soft kiss on my cheek as his soft hand touched my arm.

When I looked into his eyes, I was finding myself wanting more than I should have, as basically we had just met. I needed to take it slow as Father had instructed.

The next day I was up early, and prepared for what I wanted to believe was an adventure of a lifetime. I was right in believing this, but at that instant I didn't realize that this adventure would lead to an even bigger one before long.

Once again, the drive through the city was backed up with traffic. There was nothing I could do but sit and wait it out. I turned on my radio and as I was listening, the music was interrupted by a startling announcement.

I heard, "This programming is being interrupted by a brief announcement for now. According to the information that has been given to us, the area surrounding a small town below a mountain in Colorado is experiencing unusual activity. There are many residents in this small town who are concerned about their safety, and the town itself. We are waiting for more information before reporting anything else. We will keep you updated as more news comes in."

Maybe this was the conversation I missed after my phone call last night.

This was outrageous—and no information from the person speaking on the news broadcast about the name of the town that they were referring to. Also, it would have been nice if that person had said why the town was in danger.

By then, the traffic was moving and it wasn't long before I reached my destination at the research building.

When I entered the building, in the lobby Doctor Neil was talking to the lady that I had spoken with the day before. She looked up and waved for me to come over to her. After I was standing by her side, she said, "Malon, I want you to go with me. Since you are now employed here, you need to familiarize yourself with the building. Then I will take you to Doctor Phillips' office, where you will be working."

"Okay, and thank you again for giving me a chance at this job."

"It's all right, Malon. Learning the building is very important for an office assistant. You will be expected to do the same job as a secretary, except with more responsibility. There are exceptions, though. You will be allowed in every office and room in the building, but cannot go near or enter some of the labs. The research being done in there is highly top secret and hush-hush. Only the scientists that work here are allowed in. There are different projects and some of them are dangerous. As long as you do your job, Malon, everything will be fine."

With these words, I was very intrigued. Adam had mentioned different projects, but hadn't talked about the secret experiments.

During the tour of the building, we walked past many labs that had no windows and thick steel doors with a combination lock to secure them. This, with the fascination of my new job, made it more exciting for me. Knowing that I was working in a building with top security and projects that were not yet known to anyone other than the scientists themselves, somewhat made my job as an office assistant look important as well. I needed this job and was willing to follow all the rules, unless I had a good reason not to.

Doctor Neil had shown me the entire building. Our next stop was Doctor Phillips' office, where she assigned me to work. When we entered the office where I would be working, a tall, nice-looking older man stood, who appeared to be very business-like and to the point. Doctor Neil briefed me on more of what my job would consist of. Again, I was fascinated by everything and the part that I would contribute to the company.

When Doctor Neil left, Doctor Phillips came from his office and locked his office door behind him.

This surprised me as I had never seen anything like that before from a boss. My first thought was that even the offices contained information that needed to be secure as well as the labs. It was like working at a military reservation in Fort Knox, Kentucky.

If there was another meaning behind what Doctor Phillips was doing, red flags would be in place. Determined to do my job well, I respected Doctor Phillips' actions and stayed away from his office door. He had left, and because of Doctor Neil, I knew what my work was for the day.

The phone rang and I said, "Doctor Shawn Phillips' office."

"Malon, it's Adam. How do you like your job so far?" Adam chuckled.

"It's very interesting, Adam. Much more than I could ever imagine it would be."

"I hope that is a good thing, Malon." Adam laughed.

"Yes, it is. I am overwhelmed with all of this. The orientation from Doctor Neil was very thorough and exciting. I haven't had a chance to speak with Doctor Phillips as he left right after Doctor Neil did."

"Don't worry, Malon. You will do fine. I am on my way out of my office. Would you like company ... and coffee?"

"Adam, that would be wonderful. I'm sure you can tell that I'm somewhat nervous today."

"I will be there very soon."

It wasn't but a few minutes and Adam entered my office room with coffee and doughnuts.

"Wow, Adam, that was quick."

Again Adam laughed and said, "Nothing is too fast, or good enough for a beautiful lady like yourself, Malon."

"Adam, that is very nice of you to say. I would love it if you would call me Mylo, my nickname."

"I would love it as well, Mylo."

I could see that Adam and I were getting closer.

"I want you to be serious with me. Now that Ann has briefed you on your job, do you have any questions that I might be able to answer?"

"Adam, I can understand security in an important company such as this one, as there is a lot of different research taking place here. I would love to know what kind of research you are working on, *only* if you are allowed to tell me."

"I pretty much work alone, Mylo. I have never been included in any research projects that my father, Doctor Neil or Doctor Phillips do together in the lab. Right now, I am working with human brains."

"Wow, Adam, that sounds exciting."

"It is, and with the findings, I pass them on to my father. He has been pushing me pretty hard as my research is very important for a project that he and my grandfather started many years ago ... that, for some reason, had gone bad. He needs to fix it before it gets worse. I know that rules here state that you are not allowed in any of the labs, but it's my lab, and some day this rule will be broken. I would like to show you what I do."

"That would be great, and I would love to watch you work."

Our coffee was gone. Adam left my office room and Doctor Phillips returned. He nodded as he passed by me and entered his office.

Not realizing that he had left his door cracked when he rushed past me, he immediately picked up the phone. What I heard was mind-boggling.

"Terry, it's Shawn. I need to speak with you right away."

"Shawn, you sound frantic!"

"Yes, Terry, but that word is mild compared to all the activity that is going on in Colorado."

"Shawn, I know things have gone bad, but surely not *that* bad."

"You have no idea how bad, Terry. Things are out of control, and if it isn't stopped soon, it will all lead back to us. Plus, Terry, I need to speak to you about Adam. I'm on my way now to explain to you what I am talking about. See you in a few minutes."

"All right, Shawn. If you see Ann, tell her to come with you. She isn't in her office and isn't answering her pager."

As Doctor Phillips turned to walk toward his office door to leave, he noticed that he had left a small crack in it by mistake and knew that he had leaked out some important information to me that could be crucial. Before he walked past me, he locked his door again. At this moment, even though I knew that there was security all around me, I was starting to take this personally.

"Malon, forget what you heard if you want to keep your job," he said as he hurried out my office room door.

The conversation that he had with Doctor Belmar was very strange. Yet again, Colorado had been mentioned, and I was sure that all of this had to do with what I had heard on the radio. He brought up Adam's name in discussion with Doctor Belmar. I was curious as to why.

There was much more to the research that took place here other than rats, mice, monkeys and the human brains that Adam was working on. I was fairly sure that I could trust Adam, but not Doctor Belmar, Doctor Phillips or Doctor Neil. If I was right about this, I knew that I needed to keep my eyes and ears open as something big was happening, and if possible, I would find out whatever it was about.

Doctor Phillips didn't return to his office the rest of the day. My day here was completed. It was time for me to leave. All I wanted to do tonight was listen to the news and maybe call my father and mother again, to see what they knew about all the mystery that was involving me in it.

What I didn't know was being talked about in Doctor Belmar's office. I would have loved to have been a fly on the wall, listening.

PART TWO

8

Suspicions Were Correct

At Doctor Belmar's office, Doctor Phillips and Doctor Neil had arrived, and what they were talking about was the research that Doctor Belmar and his father did many years ago, and also Adam and I.

"Shawn, tell me what is so urgent that you felt the need to pull me away from a golf game at the club."

"Terry, don't tell me you didn't hear the announcement on the radio and television this morning."

"No, I didn't listen to the radio or television any time today."

"Terry, like I said, the research that was done years ago by your father and you is about to surface. This is not only going to affect you, but also Ann, Adam and me."

"Shawn, you are panicking for nothing. Yes, there were a few kinks in the project, but in time everything will work itself out. Okay, what has Adam done now that has you so worked up?"

"Adam is spending far too much time with my new office assistant, Malon. Have you ever talked to him about any of our projects, and the research project that we are working on now?"

"Of course not, Shawn. Adam has been working on his own research project that, hopefully, should improve what my father and I messed up years ago, that you, Ann, and I have been working on for twenty years now. As for Malon, she hasn't a clue about any of this. I have hired a man to keep an eye on her when she is at work. Even if she did suspect something, she wouldn't know what to look for."

Doctor Neil had been sitting there listening to Doctor Belmar and Doctor Phillips talk, and now she had something to say. "Terry, I forewarned you the other day in the hall to the fact that Malon's home town is Applegrove. Things are not good there, and only getting worse. If, for some reason, the name of the town is revealed on the news and she hears about everything going on there, she will be more intrigued to find out more about it. Years ago, when your father and you went there, did you tell anyone that you were working on any project in the area?"

"My father did, Ann, but he would never reveal to anyone exactly what we were doing on Sleeping Indian Mountain. You should already know that my father, Doctor Wayne Belmar, was too smart of a man and scientist to reveal any information on any research project without knowing the complete outcome of it. No one there suspected anything. There were other companies coming and going to Applegrove at the time. The research that Father and I did then, and what all three of us are doing now, will change the world. As for Malon, even if she does find out about the area, she still won't be able to connect any of what is going on there now with us. I think you both are overreacting!"

"Okay, Terry, we will continue to do it your way. We both just hope you are right."

Doctor Belmar was a highly respected and smart man. He was one of the best, or the best scientist alive in the world. Next in line was Doctor Shawn Phillips and Doctor Ann Neil.

The only thing at times better than being intelligent in the manner that all three of them were was persistence, perseverance and a country girl who needed to help her town and the many people in it. This was something that would come later.

After a phone call from Adam, and listening for hours to the same newscast as earlier, it was time to give my parents a phone call.

This time the phone just rang with no answer. I would call again after the television or radio station gave out more information. My gut told me that my suspicions were correct. They were referring to my home town, Applegrove, Colorado.

9

Evasive

After a good night's sleep, it was time to leave for the office. This morning I decided to take the subway into the city. Adam had promised me a night out for dinner and dancing. We were becoming more than just friends and getting closer every day. I knew I could talk to him about anything and everything.

While on the subway, I sat next to a couple of men who were talking about the news report. I overheard them and was paying close attention to every word that was said.

"You know, Frank, I am really not surprised that there is something weird going on in a small town in Colorado."

"Why is that, Ray? I thought you liked the state of Colorado."

"For Pete's sake, Frank, you know that I love the state of Colorado. Don't you ever listen to the news?"

"Yes, I do, but between the old woman nagging at me all the time, and my dog taking off and tearing up the neighbor's yard, there are many times when

I can't watch television. What's up with the state of Colorado?"

"Yesterday they mentioned how the community in a small town was having problems and were afraid."

"Afraid of what?"

"I have no idea, but whatever it is, it's not being told at the moment."

"Really!"

"Yes, years ago, I went to a small town there on a fishing trip. Supposed to be the time of my life. Instead, when we got there and went into a store to get our fishing licenses, we overheard a crowd of people telling stories that would scare the hair off of anyone. After that happened, we left the area to go to another town. We did some river fishing. Instead of catching a fish, I caught nothing but sticks and branches floating down the river. Worst vacation of my life!"

"That sucks," Frank said as he turned his head to smile and tried not to laugh.

By then, the subway had stopped and my walk to Wayne Belmar Research Industries was a ways away. I had to walk faster than before as I couldn't be late.

When I did enter the building, I saw the same man as I had seen the day before, sitting in a chair by the door. Yesterday, I attributed it to the possibility of him being an undercover security officer hired to watch people coming into the building, because of all the research being done there. But today he had a newspaper, and as I walked away from him, I noticed that he was watching me. As soon as he thought I couldn't see him, he got up from the chair and was walking my way.

Then I ducked into the lady's room without him seeing me. When I came out, he was gone. I realized that maybe once again my imagination was running wild, so I stopped thinking about it and kept walking to the elevator.

Unfortunately, the man was well trained and was waiting at the elevator for me. When the door opened for me, the man said, "Ladies first."

I said, "Thank you," but noticed he was walking in the same direction I was when the elevator door opened at my floor, where my office room was located.

I shrugged it off as a coincidence and opened my office door. Doctor Phillips came to my desk with papers for me to type and enter into his office computer. Once again, he was looking over his glasses at me and still checking me out.

In my mind, I was very curious as to what it was about me that Doctor Phillips didn't like or trust. I started talking to him, because I didn't like the way I felt. The reaction I got from him and his words that were said made me realize that there was no way that he was going to change the way he felt.

"Good morning, Doctor Phillips. I just want you to know that I am here on time and ready to help you in any way that I can."

"You have just started this job, Malon. Only time will tell what kind of an asset you are to this company, and to me. Just remember that whatever you overhear, or see while you are at work, stays here when you leave."

With him saying these still somewhat, non-trusting words to me, Doctor Phillips walked away. He had given me instructions on a paper of what my job was for the day.

All of this was starting to become very strange to me. The expression on Doctor Neil's face when she read that I was from Applegrove, Colorado. Also the words of Doctor Terry Belmar, the conversation I overheard from Doctor Neil as she spoke with Doctor Belmar, the one I once again overheard from Doctor Phillips, the man in the lobby that appeared to be following me, and the distrust of Doctor Phillips as he spoke with me just now.

Again, I needed to speak to Adam. If anyone would know anything about all of this, I believed that he would. I called his office.

"Doctor Adam Belmar, please."

"Doctor Adam is not in his office right now. I will put you through to his answering machine," Diane, Adam's office assistant, replied.

I left him a message to call me right back as soon as he could.

Meanwhile, in Adam's father's office, Adam was sitting with his father at the desk, discussing the research that he had been working on in his lab.

"Okay, Adam, the paper that you handed me

will be looked over and discussed by Shawn, Ann and myself. You have explored and researched so many avenues of it that maybe we will now have what we are looking for."

"I have spent many hours on it, Father. Not knowing exactly why you keep pushing me to research the behavior pattern of so many brains makes me wonder what this project that you are working on is really all about."

"Adam, you know that even though you are my son, this research is very pertinent in the other research that Shawn, Ann and I have been working on. This was a research project that your grandfather and I started many years ago. Since then, there have been several new developments and problems are starting to occur. This is why we need answers now."

Adam knew that his father was being still very evasive with him and wasn't going to give him a straight answer, but he said, "All right, Father, I will keep the research going until you completely find what you are looking for."

Adam got up from his chair and left his father's office. Planning a return to his lab, he stopped by his office to see if he had business to take care of there first.

Diane told him that he had a message. After checking it, he was on his way to talk to me. I had gotten up from my desk to file some papers when Adam walked through my office door with a cardboard carrier containing two cups of coffee.

10

No Expectations

"Adam, you are here."

"Yes, and I even brought us coffee."

"Just before you walked in, I was thinking about walking down to the cafeteria to get a cup."

"Glad I could help, Milo."

"Me too, Adam. Actually, maybe you can help me even more. I am wondering now if my working here is such a good idea."

"Why, Mylo? I thought that everything was going fairly well with your job."

"I have suspicions that I am being followed by a man here in the building. Also, Doctor Phillips and Doctor Neil are concerned about what I might find out, or overhear, while I am working."

"I'm not sure what you are talking about. Please explain."

I told Adam what I had seen and overheard. Adam started talking and told me something that I didn't expect to hear.

"Mylo, I, too, have questions about some of the research that has gone on here for many years. When my father was working with my grandfather ...

one day, when I was very young … I came here with my father. He left me in his office and told me to stay there and wait for him to return. I told him I would, but after a couple hours, I went looking for him. I went to his lab and opened the door. If Father saw me, I would have been punished. So I hid.

"On several tables I saw something that I couldn't understand. In there were several huge metal boxes. Also, I saw my grandfather putting something in a test tube. As I continued to hide, I saw what I thought to be clouds coming from the boxes. It wasn't long, and I could barely see at all. I started for the door to sneak out of there and my father caught me. He told me that whatever I saw in there was a *secret* and not to tell anyone about it. I didn't, and grew up with this secret … until now."

"Now that you are a scientist yourself, Adam, what do you think their research was?"

"I have thought about it about many times, but to this day, I still don't know. It could be that they were researching clouds, or maybe fog, and how to stop or control them. I just know that after I snuck in there that day, my grandfather changed things and had thick doors installed on all the labs. Now, in order to get into one of them, a code is used before the door will open, either going into or coming out of each lab."

"Why do you think all of them find me a threat to their research, Adam?"

"Once again, Mylo, I honestly don't know. Why the state of Colorado is bothering them is very strange indeed. Because of this, I am going to make sure that you and I are seen together here more than we have been. I don't think that anyone will harm you. No one here wants to lose their job.

"Together ... we are going to work together. You need answers to your questions, and I need answers to mine. My father has kept them from me long enough on so many levels of why, exactly, I have been researching so many human brains for months now. I know that this has nothing to do with medical advancement. It all falls back on some project that my father and grandfather started years ago. I have tried more than once to find out what they are working on in Father's lab, and the secret is hidden in my father's mind."

"Do the scientists here do research for the government?"

"At times we have done research on many animals. If that is what is going on now, I haven't been told anything about it."

I had learned many things today. I was right about Adam. He had told me things that he should have kept to himself, but out of being comfortable with me, he chose to share what he knew. There was more going on in this research building than I probably ever could have imagined. With Adam by my side, and watching over me, I felt as if both of us would uncover the secrets that Doctor Belmar, Doctor Phillips and Doctor Neil had been keeping and trying to hide for many years.

While we were talking, the three doctors were

working in the lab.

Doctor Neil walked over to a table and lifted up a sheet. As she did this, she said, "Terry, I think the project and specimen are coming along nicely."

"Maybe what *you* see, Ann, but we still need to go over the research from Adam before we can complete this," Terry replied.

"Terry, I need to ask you again if you have told Adam anything about this," said Doctor Phillips.

"No, Shawn! This was something that my father and I agreed on just days before he passed away. Adam is a great scientist, and yes, my son. But he would never let me complete this project if he knew anything about it!" Terry said with a firm voice.

"Do you really think that Adam's new friend won't try to find out information on the research here?" Shawn asked.

"As long as you and Ann keep your mouths shut, Malon and Adam will not find out anything. When we get the research project perfect, the whole world will know about it, and who created it."

Enough had been said, and all three of them continued to work.

Adam and I left Doctor Phillips' office. I was leaving for the day. In the lobby sat the man that I believed was following me. He saw Adam with me and continued to sit in the chair and pretend to read a magazine. The only way that Adam could talk to this man was if he caught him in the fact. We left the building.

At the restaurant, Adam sat closer to me and held my hand as we listened to the band and waited for our dinner. A few times, as we gazed into each other's eyes, I thought that Adam was going to kiss me. Then he would smile and look away or down at the table. I could see that he was waiting on me to lean his way when he was looking at me.

When we returned to my hotel door before I unlocked it, he leaned slightly closer to me. At that time, I also leaned toward him, and we kissed. It was magic, and wonderful.

When he left, after making sure that I was safely in my hotel room, my thoughts were not just on Adam, but with no expectations of Adam and I having a future together. I also wondered what Doctor Belmar would say about Adam and my kiss.

In days to come, would the three doctors start to trust me? The outcome was near, and before long the secrets and truth would be known.

It was time for me to call my father again in the morning. This time, hopefully Father and Mother would be home.

11

Help Needed

Morning came too early for me on a Saturday. My intent to sleep in didn't happen.

As I lay in bed, my thoughts turned to Adam and the kiss we shared. The reality was that I really hadn't been in the city long enough to call it home, as my intentions when I came here were to work for a while, see how city life was, and return to my home town. Now that Adam might be a part of my life, the direction of my thoughts could change.

Sitting on the edge of my bed, I dialed my home number. After five rings, I was ready to hang up when I heard my father's voice.

"Father, hello."

"Mylo?"

"Yes, Father. Can you hear me?"

"I barely can. There are a lot of problems with the phone lines right now."

"Are you and Mother okay?"

"Yes, Mylo, we are fine."

"I heard something on the news about havoc in Colorado. Is it close to you?"

"Yes. We are both safe."

"Can you tell me what is going on there?"

Once again, I could hear crackling and static on the phone.

"Father, are you there?"

"Barely, Mylo. Before we get disconnected, I need to tell you something. Can you hear me?"

"Yes."

"After our last talk, I did some checking on the name of the two men that came here years ago to research Sleeping Indian Mountain. Out of coincidence, according to old motel records, it was Wayne Belmar and Terry Belmar. The other day, when you told me who you were working for, I continued to think about it. I remembered the men by their faces, but not their names. You were with me that day when they stopped at the ranch to ask directions."

"That is strange, Father, as the night that Adam introduced me to his father, I had a feeling that I had seen him before. Did you find out what they were doing there?"

"No. They did their research and left. Although, they were pulling a huge boxed-in trailer behind a big Suburban."

"Do you need me there now, Father?"

"No! Not now, Mylo!"

Before I could ask anything else, the phone connection was gone.

Now the pieces of the puzzle were starting to fit. The name of my home town, state and the research done on Sleeping Indian Mountain. This is why they all looked at me as being a threat to them.

Somehow, the secret that Doctor Terry Belmar had in his lab that day, when Adam went in there, had to be a secret about the mountain.

Not feeling very good about the last words my father said to me, I sat on the edge of my bed with my head in my hands, battling with myself on whether I should leave Adam and Wayne Belmar Research Industries and go back home, in spite of what my father said.

Respecting my father, his wisdom and thoughts on anything he told me, was and had been my number one priority. There was a huge reason why Father told me to stay here. From the newscast, everyone there in Applegrove and the surrounding area felt as if they were in danger. Something, or someone, had instilled fear in them. This would be a conversation that I would keep to myself for now, until I had more answers.

When I was growing up, Rocky and I explored the mountain almost every day. Back then, there was no fear in a small country town. Over the years, things had changed, and everyone was terrorized. What could it be?

Without Rocky, it was time for me to investigate the secrets contained inside the research building where I worked—on my own.

Another question that came to mind was, why would a big research company from New York City travel all the way to Applegrove, Colorado, pulling a huge trailer full of whatever?

Why would Doctor Terry Belmar be so evasive

with his own son?

After thinking about all of this, I had to come up with a plan to find out what the three doctors were working on in the lab, and also find a way to get in there without being seen. Even though I trusted Adam, I couldn't involve him in what I needed to do.

That night back home, Mother and Father were talking.

"Allen, what are we going to do? We are losing cattle, and each night you are sitting in front of the back door, waiting for whatever those things are, to try to enter our home!"

"No, Mindy, I won't give in to this. I know all of us are afraid, as whatever this is won't stop, and they are coming from the mountain. Every person in the other towns that are close by are standing our ground until we know what we are up against and can find a way to fight them."

"We aren't getting help from anyone, as Sleeping Indian Mountain is so cloudy and foggy that no one can land up there. They would need to come in on the top of the mountain with a helicopter."

"I know that none of us men can go up there either. We will wait it out, like I said. Meanwhile, if Mylo calls and, for some reason, I am not here, choose what words you use when speaking to her as we *can't* tell her what we have seen or heard. We need her to stay safe."

"Don't worry, Allen, I won't tell her anything but good thoughts."

If I would have known what Mother and Father were saying, I probably would have disregarded my plans and gone home, but in the end, I knew that it was better that I waited, like Father told me to.

The research building was off limits for me for a couple of days, and there was no way for me to get in. This would give me the time I needed to set my plan in motion.

12

Action and Maybe Reaction

It was Monday morning and I was ready to go to my office. I would take things in steps and start my own personal research project.

Today I drove to work instead of taking the subway. It was going to be a long day.

As I entered the building, I noticed the same man sitting on a chair close to the front door. I was sure then that one of the three doctors was having him tail me. As I walked past him, he got up from his chair and walked behind me toward the elevator. To his dismay, he came to an abrupt halt when one of the workers in the building pushed a big cart in front of him. He had to stop and couldn't get around it.

Walking faster, I ducked into an empty room, cracking the door just enough so as to watch and see what he did. When he walked past the room, he looked frantic. He couldn't find me. As he walked past the door leading to the stairs, I left the room.

I climbed the stairs as fast as I could. Apparently, the man kept taking the elevator up and down each floor, looking for me. Things couldn't have been timed better, as when I opened the door to the floor that I worked on, I could hear Doctor Phillips talking.

"What do you think you are doing?"

"Is that girl in there?" the man asked.

Doctor Phillips, with a disgusted look on his face, said, "You know damn good and well that she isn't!"

"Really, Doctor Phillips, it wasn't my fault. Some worker pushed a cart in front of me in the lobby. I couldn't catch up with her after that. I checked everywhere!" the man said with a worried look on his face.

"This is not good! You were hired to watch her every move in here. For your sake, you better hope that she shows up here soon. As of now, you are no longer employed here. Leave this building immediately!" Doctor Phillips said as he pointed his finger at the man's face.

"*You* can't fire me. Doctor Belmar hired me. Not you!"

"I already talked to Doctor Belmar about things going bad where you are concerned, watching her. He was forewarned that I would take over if I needed to. *Get out of the building now!*" Doctor Phillips said, yelling at the top of his lungs.

The man never said another word. I shut the door to the stairs after he walked past me. With him gone, and no one to replace him for now, my plan was going in the right direction. Because of what was said, it was all the proof I needed to hear that they all believed that I was definitely a threat to them and their work.

I shut the stairs door, and walked down the hall to the office. When I opened the door, I could see that Doctor Phillips was putting a paper into the file cabinet. Something he didn't want me to see, as he looked around the room.

Not wanting him to suspect that I knew anything at all, I smiled and said, "Good morning, Doctor Phillips. Sorry I am a little late."

"Malon, this is not acceptable around here. *Don't* let it happen again," Doctor Phillips said firmly.

Again I smiled at him, and told him I would make sure I was on time from then on.

He turned around and walked into his office. This time, making sure that his office door was completely shut. I could hear him say, "Terry, my guess was right." He was calling Doctor Terry Belmar, to tell him that he had fired the man that lost me in the lobby.

Not being able to hear anything I wanted to this time, I followed Doctor Phillips, to overhear anything that might help me with my research project. The way I also looked at it was this. Turn around is fair play. They distrusted me because they were hiding something. I needed to find out what it was, so it was my turn to follow them, like the man who hid out in the lobby of the building did, until I entered each day. He had been following me. Now, in my way, I was giving back to them what was given to me.

In a short time, Doctor Phillips came out of his

office. Not saying a word to me, he left.

Giving him a short time to walk ahead of me, I left as well. Ducking in and out of empty rooms, hoping that he and Doctor Belmar would be talking where I could hear them instead of the lab, or Doctor Belmar's office.

I was rounding a corner of a hallway and I hit a triple header. With Doctor Belmar was Doctor Neil. When Doctor Phillips approached them, harsh words were said.

"Terry, you really hired a winner to keep an eye on Malon. Today he lost her in the lobby, so I fired him."

"What?" Ann said as Terry looked down at the floor with his arms crossed.

"Yes, I did. I also told him that he was to leave the building, and hope that Malon showed up in her office room. The last thing we need, Terry, is for her to snoop around. I told you before that with Malon working here, and her home town being Applegrove, Colorado, that none of this is going to turn out good!" Shawn answered as he also crossed his arms.

"Terry, I, too, feel uncomfortable about her working here. I wish I wouldn't have hired her," Ann commented.

"You two amaze me!" said Dr. Belmar. "You are so busy concentrating on your doubts, instead of the fact that we are getting closer to having our research perfected. The only way that Malon could be a threat to us is if you two keep acting funny around her. As for that man I hired, Shawn, I will go along with you firing him this time, but from now on, remember who owns this building, and who you are both working for! I will hire someone else, if it will pacify the two of you. My son has been occupying a lot of her time. I am fairly sure he is all she is thinking about now."

Doctor Belmar let both doctors know that he was irritated with them, but also who they were dealing with, not just working with him, but who they were working for.

"If you are sure about this, Terry," Ann replied with a questioning look on her face.

"I am sure, Ann."

"Okay, Terry, but I still don't trust her. We all have our jobs and our lives at stake."

"This research needs to be completed soon," Shawn said while Ann was shaking her head up and down, agreeing with him.

Afraid of being seen, I walked softly down the hall to my office room. After entering, I sat down at my desk to make it look like I had been working.

It wasn't but a few minutes and Doctor Phillips walked through the door. I knew that he was checking on me.

Everything again had been confirmed. Questioning, and wanting to know what Doctor Phillips had on the paper that he'd slipped into a locked old file cabinet, was—I knew—something that had to pertain to the research in the lab. I had a gut feeling about it.

The hard part was getting the key and unlocking it so I could see what he was afraid for me to know.

He always kept this file cabinet key in his office. He locked the office door every time he left to go to the lab, or when he left for the day.

Somehow, I would find a way to get the key.

I knew that Doctor Phillips would do anything he thought he needed to do to keep the secrets that Doctor Belmar's lab held. Also, that meant that Doctor Neil would go along with it. I didn't know for sure, but believed that they might be dangerous if it came down to either them or me. I had to be sure of every action I took, as there could be a serious reaction.

13

Reliving a Meeting

Doctor Phillips left for the lab.

The phone rang and this time it was Adam, checking to see if I was all right. My next plan was in motion. I called a locksmith, pretending to be a scientist in that office and had misplaced the key to the old file cabinet. I was going to have him make me another key.

I was told that he could make one. I told him to bypass the lady at the front desk and come to my office. I gave him directions.

Now the wait for the locksmith. This would turn bad for me if this plan failed. I was told that he wasn't far away and would be here soon. I put on one of Doctor Phillips' lab jackets and sat at my desk, waiting. It was a short time and I heard a tap on my office room door. It was him. I went to the door and told him I was Doctor Thomas.

As the old man shifted through all the old keys that he had for many years, I was starting to get worried that he may not find anything that might be a match or close to it. Then suddenly, I heard him say, "I found a match, Doctor Thomas. This is one of the oldest file cabinets that I have ever seen or worked with."

A feeling of relief and anticipation came over me. It was not long and he had made a key. I paid him. He handed me the key and left.

When he shut the door, I took off the lab coat and placed it where I had found it. Things couldn't have gone smoother than it did for me. I had the key in my hand and what was needed to unlock a few secrets that I knew had been hidden for many years.

A part of me wanted to look inside it now, but I was afraid that because it was late in the day, someone would stop by the office to check on me. Then I would get caught. I would get my chance soon enough.

I opened my hand that held the odd-shaped key, and stared at it. As I held this key, I drifted back in my mind to everything I had heard about me, the town, the state I came from, and everything that had been said. Also what my father had said.

A lot had been accomplished on my first day of researching the secret that Doctor Belmar, Doctor Phillips and Doctor Neil were hiding from Adam, and maybe the world.

I closed my hand and put the key in a small pocket in my handbag. Soon after, Doctor Phillips opened the door. He definitely didn't trust me. This time I smiled at him and started typing. I was making him believe that I had been busy all day.

After Doctor Phillips saw me working, he turned around to walk out of my office door again.

I had accomplished what I'd set out to do that day. Tomorrow would be the day I would search each paper and item that was buried in the old file cabinet.

My day of working was done and it was time to leave, to meet Adam for dinner and dancing at our favorite place.

When I entered the lobby to leave the building, there was no one watching me. My thoughts were that now was not the time to be careless. If any of the three knew what I had done, or was about to do, I would be fired, or someone else would be hired to watch my every move again. With Doctor Belmar believing that I was just focusing on Adam, I had the reason I needed.

Later in the evening, Adam told me to meet him on the same bench where he had met me a few days ago. It was a warm, beautiful evening, and being a romantic, I couldn't wait to see what he had planned for me.

As I walked up to him, he said, "Mylo, would you like a hotdog?"

This made me smile and my words were, "Of course, Adam. I would love one."

He had shown me that he, too, was a romantic and wanted to relive that day we'd met. We continued to talk as we ate, and then we took the same ride through Central Park with a horse-drawn carriage. This time, Adam had his arm around me as we laughed and pointed at different things we saw.

The warm air had turned cool. As he stood

beside me at my car, he took my hands in his and kissed me good night. When I was safely in my car, he walked away. I was so happy that this day had gone so well.

14

Big News Stopped

The next morning I was able to walk to my office room without feeling as if someone was watching me. Doctor Phillips looked at the clock when I walked through the door. He never said a word. Instead, he pulled his glasses down on his nose some, and looked over the top of them at me.

I smiled and once again wished him a good morning and good day. I had to act like everything was good, and that I was only there to work. How little did he know that my handbag contained a key, in hopes of being able to destroy him, Doctor Belmar and Doctor Neil.

Once again when he left my office room, he locked his door to his office. He was leaving, hopefully, for the whole day.

With me wanting to give him ample time away from his office, I sat at my desk and continued to type. My guess was that he might pretend to leave and come back to check on me.

After a couple of hours, either he was very busy in the lab or had gone to talk to one of the other doctors. The thought of him planning a sneak attack did enter my mind.

Today, though, my plan was to open the locked old file cabinet, to look through it as much as I could get by with, until I got nervous about being caught again. I had no idea what all was kept in there. The right time was set and I had to make sure that everything that came out of it went back in the same way.

Still being somewhat nervous, I walked to open my door, and listened to hear if anyone was coming down the hallway. Hearing nothing, I shut the door softly and walked across the room to see what I could find in the cabinet.

As I opened it, and not sure what was hidden in it, the paper that I believed Doctor Phillips put in there was sitting on top. When I turned it over, my imagination went wild. It wasn't a normal paper that someone would file. What I saw was a copy of an obituary for a man who had passed away in the city very recently.

I set the paper aside and continued to look. I found more of the same pages of many people who had passed away. Most of these people had been at the same mortuary in the city.

This definitely was not what I expected. Why would Doctor Phillips want copies of people's obituaries? As I looked through them, I saw that they were dated back many years ago, and some were recent. There was so much I didn't know, but I knew I could find the missing pieces and make them fit the puzzle.

There were other pages with names and dates in the old cabinet. This I knew was important to solving this secret. As I continued to read the dates, names and places of the deaths of the deceased, it felt like I had a pit in the bottom of my stomach. Not all of them came from the city. Some were from Applegrove, dated back to when I was a kid.

Before long, after I had more information, Adam would be told about all of this. Doctor Terry might want to keep him in the dark, but I wasn't about to.

I took the page with dates and names and started to sort through the copies of the obituaries. I wanted to see if there was a connection. There was, and again I was confused as to why Doctor Phillips had this information. I wanted to think about it and regroup. This might take a while as the secrets hidden there were now my treasures.

Doctor Phillips had been gone for a long time. Afraid that I would get caught, I started arranging things in the order of where I had removed them. When the recent page was set in the exact spot it came from, I closed the drawer and locked it. The key went into my handbag. I had a lot of thinking to do.

Next was to finish my work before Doctor Phillips returned. I had, in two days of my personal research, accomplished and found pertinent infor-mation that should have been known many years ago. A question was, why was this old file cabinet in *here* instead of Doctor Terry Belmar's office? I felt like I was gaining ground and didn't want to over-think my ideas.

As I finished my work, Doctor Neil came through my office door. She could see that I was working and asked, "Malon, is Doctor Phillips in his office?"

"No, he left early this morning after handing me my work for the day."

"I'm assuming he is still in the building. I will call him on his pager. I may not be able to get through to him, so if you are still here when he returns, tell him I need to speak to him immediately."

Something serious was on her mind as when she walked away, she looked frantic.

I called Adam and told him that I was tired from the day of work and would see him tomorrow after work. I had so much to sort out tonight and think about.

When I left the research building, I was walking down the sidewalk of the city and stopped at a news stand to buy a current newspaper. My reasoning behind this was to check out the obituary column and see if Doctor Phillips provided a current page daily to the old file cabinet. His reasoning for doing this was more than I could fathom.

As far as I could see, the big news of Applegrove had stopped. Father told me things were bad there. I felt like because it was a small town, maybe the city of New York was disregarding it.

Regardless of what they did, my research would continue until all of my questions, doubts and needs of making sure that my family, friends and the community that I was born and raised in were safe from the Wayne Belmar Research Industries, and that Doctor Terry Belmar, Doctor Shawn Phillips and Doctor Ann Neil were found out by the world for what I believed was harmful to society.

They would all pay for what they had done—and were doing.

15

Stay Safe Back Home

Back in Applegrove, the entire community showed up for a meeting at the town hall. The city council wanted to have a meeting with the mayor.

The mayor started talking, and this is what he said: "We are all here today to discuss our town and what we need to do about all of this strange behavior, and the losses we have all experienced. Sam, I want you to speak first. It seems like you and your family have had more misfortune than any of us so far."

Sam stood up with tears in his eyes. "Thank you, John. The worst loss I have suffered was losing my wife, Mary. We would have celebrated our thirtieth wedding anniversary last week.

"The day that I found her lying on the ground in a puddle of blood next to the barn, with her throat torn out of her neck, I wanted to die. Yesterday, I buried her on the mountain. It was so foggy, I could barely see to drive up there, but since that was the place she wanted to be buried at, and rest for eternity, I didn't care what happened to me, or if I made it back down from the mountain alive or not. While I was there, I dug Mary's grave.

"I know that all of you wanted to be there as every one of you loved her, but I wasn't going to put any of your lives at risk as well as my own. When all of this is over, we will have a real funeral for her. The day she was attacked, I had come into town to buy more hay for my livestock and didn't get back until after dark. She must have got tired of wondering where the sounds were coming from, and went out to see for herself what was outside. Anyway, like all of you—besides losing Mary—I, too, lost cattle, horses, chickens and pigs."

Sam sat down with tears still streaming from his eyes. In fact, after hearing about Mary, everyone there was crying. Even the mayor and the town council.

"Next, I would like for a raise of hands of anyone else who would like to speak," the mayor said as he took out a handkerchief from his shirt pocket to wipe away tears from his eyes.

"Allen, please stand."

"Thank you, John. Like all of you, I, too, have lost most of my stock. For years, all of us would find an animal dead and attribute it to wolves, a lion, bobcat or a bear. I can tell you that Mindy and I saw something years ago that frightened us. One night, my daughter Mylo's horse was killed. All of us were in bed and we heard a noise. I went outside, and with my flashlight, was looking around everywhere to see where the noise was coming from.

"Mindy waited as long as she could for me to return, but after a while, out of fear for me, she came outside with her rifle to find me. She saw the light shining from the flashlight and came up behind me. That night we saw some people who had torn clothes that were bent over Mylo's horse, eating his throat from the outside in, tearing the flesh and pulling it away from his neck.

"This was outrageous. After discussing this years ago, even though this was strange and out of the ordinary behavior, that maybe it might have been people without a home that were hungry and saw Mylo's horse lying dead on the ground ... we didn't report it, and probably should have. In fact, when we talked to our daughter because of the graphics that we saw that night, we didn't even tell *her* all the details.

"Over the years, things have become much worse here. The National Guard won't fly into the area and land on top of Sleeping Indian Mountain because of all the clouds and fog. As you know, this is where all of us know where this evil is coming from. The road is steep, with many curves. We are not sure exactly what is *on* Sleeping Indian, or how many we all might find up there. We could be out-numbered. I know that a bunch of us in this room have experienced some things that have curled our toes, and we all have our own thoughts on what is doing this.

"It is getting late, John, and before long it will be dark. Can we please talk more about this on a different day?" Father asked.

"Yes, Allen. Our town meeting is over with for

now. Go home and stay safe," the mayor replied.

Yet in the city at that time, while I sat in front of the television, watching the news, they showed a mortuary that was burning down that the reporter was focused on. There had been an explosion and the reporter was talking about it either being an act of arson or a leaking gas line.

The name of this mortuary was King's Mortuary. By coincidence, that was the same morgue listed on the obituary pages in the file cabinet.

My mind was out of control with trying to make heads or tails out of all this information. Did I think that the mortuary had caught on fire by itself? No, I did not!

I wanted to share it with Father and Mother, but didn't want them to worry about me. They needed to stay safe back home. There would come a time later when I could talk to them about it. For them, staying safe was something they were struggling with. Eventually, all of what I learned from my research and personal investigation would make complete sense to me.

For now, I still had work to do in the old file cabinet. I would know soon what I'd been looking for, and wouldn't stop until I had all the information I needed to put an end to all the secrets that started in the lab and ended up on Sleeping Indian Mountain.

16

Surprise For Everyone

The next day I went to work wearing a smile when I saw Doctor Phillips. As usual, he was his cold self. All he did was look at me and hand me more papers to type. The pages were always something that I couldn't understand.

When he walked out the door, I knew that maybe I might get more information if I followed him again. I was right. Doctor Neil was on her way to Doctor Phillips' office when she met up with him in the hall.

Ann asked, "Where were you yesterday afternoon?"

"I took care of the business you and I talked about. Terry told me to do it. He said that very soon Adam will have all the kinks and imperfections that weren't working in the human brains perfect again. At that time, we will have it all perfected. We have everything that we need already in the labs, other than the brains for now."

"Are you sure you destroyed it, Shawn? I mean, we are talking about our lives here, and careers. It isn't that I don't believe Terry, because I do, but here lately, I feel that he has made some really careless decisions," Ann replied to Shawn.

"If you are referring to Malon, and trusting her, I am in complete agreement with you. There is something about her smile every day that makes me wonder what she is thinking, or up to. Before long, we may have to take things into our own hands."

With this being said, I knew I had to not only be more careful than I had been, but also finish getting information and go to Adam with all of it. He deserved to know everything his father, grand-father, Doctor Phillips and Doctor Neil had done and were doing.

As I quietly left and went back to my office room, I waited to see if Doctor Phillips returned. This time I waited three hours as I typed the papers he wanted me to. When I suspected that Doctor Phillips had gone to the lab with Doctor Neil, I returned to the cabinet to open it, after checking to make sure that no one was coming down the hall.

Very carefully, I unlocked and opened it. I removed the pages that had been copied from the obituary columns. Today I was going to check the names and places of those who had passed away more so than I had before.

As I looked through each one, I saw several that came from Applegrove and one that really stuck out in my mind. The name on that one was Amy Belmar. She had passed away many years ago. Was this Doctor Terry Belmar's wife? I made several copies for myself of what I had picked out, and knew

I couldn't look more in depth here at the office. Another item that I found was a set of old keys that may have been used years ago to enter each lab. Again out of fear, I put everything back, closed and locked the cabinet. I had what I needed for now, and put them in my desk.

As I sat there typing, Doctor Terry Belmar entered the room. I had stopped and put things back at the right moment.

"Good afternoon, Malon. I left Doctor Phillips in the lab an hour ago, and he told me he was coming back here soon. Have you seen him?"

"No, I haven't. Is there a message you would like me to give him if he does return?"

"No, I will talk to him tomorrow, Malon. I am going to the club to play golf. If you talk to Adam today, would you tell him that he needs to meet with me tomorrow morning?"

"Yes, I will be talking to Adam later tonight and will tell him."

"All right. Later, Malon."

"Later, Doctor Belmar."

My typing was ready for Doctor Phillips to review. If he didn't come back soon, I would enter it into the office computer. I wanted to leave and get out of the building before he did return. I had many copies to take home with me that day.

He never returned and I entered what I needed to. I rushed out the door, walking fast, and checking to see if anyone was watching me. As I left the building, I went straight to my car with a sigh of relief.

At the hotel room I turned on the television. The news reporter was talking. The investigation about the mortuary was still in progress. From what they had found so far, it looked more like arson than a leaking gas line. As I sat there, adding another piece to this puzzle of secrets, I was very convinced that burning the morgue down was part of Doctor Terry Belmar's, Doctor Shawn Phillips' and Doctor Ann Neil's plan to destroy the morgue records, and the other information that they were afraid of someone seeing, to lead all the insanity back to them.

Something kept telling me I needed to fly home. What I had acquired, and what I saw or heard from Father and the townspeople, would help to give me an insight on all of this.

I knew that Adam was working extra hard right now, to finish his research. Doctor Belmar was pushing him to finish up. This weekend would be perfect. By then, I would know more here and be able to find out more in Applegrove.

This would have to be a surprise for my parents, as I knew they would only try to discourage me from coming.

I called the airline and booked a flight that also included a rental car. All I could tell Adam for now was that I was homesick and would be flying back to the city on Sunday. This was not totally a lie, as I really did miss my parents. Applegrove was my roots, and even with everything bad going on there, I also missed my friends and all the people in the town.

Rocky and I had shared a lot of history on the old mountain. If I could save lives and make Sleeping Indian Mountain safe again, all of this would be worth it. The more I heard, found and read about, the more I felt that all of this started many years ago with Doctor Terry Belmar and his father, Doctor Wayne Belmar.

Before long, the secrets of the mountain would all be exposed and life could start once again for all the people that I care about and love.

PART THREE

17

Home Again

Since it was the last day of the work week, I was prepared for anything else that I was searching for to solve this mystery.

Doctor Phillips was leaving my office room when I arrived. My papers to type for the day were already waiting for me on my desk. Today I had an early plane to catch, so would do my work first, and then try to look in the old file cabinet for one more clue before leaving.

As I was busy typing, Adam was busy talking to his father in Doctor Belmar's office.

"Adam, how close are you to being done?"

"I am very close, Father. You told me that my research would help change the way everyone looks at the world. That's great, but where did you find all the human brains I have been correcting and working on? I have them as good as they are going to get. By the first part of this coming week, they will be done."

"That is wonderful, Adam. The brains are from parts that have been donated to research," Doctor Belmar told Adam as he looked away. He couldn't even look at his own son as he knew what he was telling him was a lie.

"If you want to include me in your lab, I would love to assist you, Shawn and Ann," Adam replied. He was sure the answer would be no, but wanted to check first. For many years he had felt like his father was covering up something. All Adam wanted from his father was the truth.

"Sorry, Adam. This research project is more advanced than you would understand. I know you are a great scientist, but this started with your grandfather and me. The next research we do, I will include you, too. Now, go finish up your project."

Adam left his father's office with the same questions as he had for years. He returned to his lab to resume his work.

I had finished my work and, after checking the hall for any soon-to-be visitors that could come through my office door at any time, I opened the file cabinet one last time. This time, after I reached into it and lifted out all the copies of the many obituaries, I happened to notice something that looked like it might be a hidden compartment at the bottom.

I took a small screwdriver from my desk and worked very carefully with it, so as not to break it, but be able to open it. When the little flap was open, in front of me was also a copy of Doctor Wayne Belmar's obituary, folded just enough to slip in there. Realizing that maybe even Doctor Phillips might be keeping this from Doctor Belmar himself, and Doctor Neil.

All I could think about was that he had his own

secret that maybe even Doctor Neil didn't know about. Also, why again was Doctor Belmar's old file cabinet in here? Still, like Adam, I had so many questions. There would be a day when the secrets hidden would surface and I couldn't wait for that day to come. It was getting closer.

At last I was done there, and as I left the Wayne Belmar Research Industries building, I carried a bag that contained all the copies I had made of all the obituaries from the file cabinet. Nothing of importance would be left behind for anyone to find and look at. I wanted my father to see what I had discovered.

As my airplane left the ground, I felt a sense of relief. I would miss Adam, but the thought of going home again made me smile. Two hours later, I was boarding another plane to take me to a town in Colorado, where I could rent a car to drive the rest of the way home. In just a couple of hours, my mother and father would have their only child with them again—at least for a couple of days.

After unloading, I got my rental car. When I drove away, I looked in the direction of my small town. The air was clean and fresh, but a huge cloud hovered in the sky that could be seen for many miles.

As I got closer to Applegrove, the clouds and fog increased and looked like a scene out of an old horror movie, where a woman was driving down a country road before dark and, all of a sudden, out of nowhere comes a man wearing a black cape. The woman swerved, who was startled by this to try to miss him. She goes off the road to find the man kneeling over the top of her, getting ready to sink his sharp, ugly, long pointed teeth into her neck.

I knew this wasn't going to happen, but locked all the doors anyway.

Soon after reliving the old movie from years ago, I reached my home. My mother's car and my father's truck were there. I knew this was going to be a big surprise for them.

After parking the car in the garage, I saw my father coming out of the porch door. He couldn't see that it was me with the different car in the garage. As Father reached the car, I climbed out and asked him, "Would you like some company?"

Father smiled and pulled me close to him. "Mylo, I am so happy to see you. But why did you come home now?"

"I had to, Father. I have been worried sick about you and Mother. Our last phone conversation was cut short from the phone lines being messed up. I have been doing some personal research of my own and have more to talk to you about, and also something to show you. I will be here until Sunday morning, and then will go back to the city for now," I replied as we walked onto the porch, where Mother stood, waiting to give me a hug.

After many tears, we entered the house. I had made it home once again, just in time for supper.

That night we just talked about the sights of the city, all the people that live there and, of course,

Adam. By the end of the day, I watched as my father went to take his rifle out of his gun case.

"Father, why are you getting your gun?"

"I might need it to protect all of you, Mylo. A lot has happened since you left. I didn't want you to know about it, as I wanted you to stay safe in the city. Then, because of all the events that are happening, you heard it on the news. All of us in this area have been waiting for the clouds and fog to lift, so that the National Guard can land on top of Sleeping Indian Mountain, to see what is up there. I'm happy you made it to the house, as the Governor has declared this area unsafe and has been broadcasting for everyone to stay home, unless it is an emergency to go into town."

"Father, in the morning, I have information that I want to share with you. Maybe you can help me figure out the secrets I have uncovered so far."

"I know you are tired, Mylo. Go sleep in your bed and we will talk tomorrow morning."

Father was right. I was tired, and my mind was stuck on working overtime. What had happened to Sleeping Indian Mountain? What was so horrific that instilled fear in an entire community and surrounding areas for many people?

I kissed Mother and Father good night, and walked to my bedroom. I stood at the window once again, wishing I could see Rocky grazing in the pasture. Father was right. So much had changed.

How I wished I could go back in years and explore the mountain without fear.

18

Stories of Fear

When I woke up in my own bed the next morning, briefly I thought that maybe I should stay in Applegrove instead of returning to the city. If I hadn't met Adam and found information that would save this area, I would have given it more thought.

I stretched, climbed out of bed, put on my robe and walked down the hall to the kitchen to get a cup of coffee. To my surprise, I saw my father hunched over his chair with his rifle across his lap, in his hands as he slept. This upset me. Father heard me in the kitchen, woke up and sat up in his chair.

"Good morning, Mylo. Hope you slept well."

"I did, Father. Do you sleep in your chair like that every night?" I asked.

"Yes, I have done this for many nights. Hopefully, it will end soon."

"Is Mother still sleeping?"

At that time, she entered the kitchen.

"We are so pleased to have you with us for a couple of days," Mother said with a huge smile.

"It's so good to be here. My time in the city is limited, so it won't be long before I come back home to stay to help you and Father with the ranch."

"We hope there is a ranch for you to come back to, Mylo. Everyone is concerned about theirs as well," Father said as he got up from his chair.

"If things are the way I believe they are, this will be over with soon," I replied.

"Mylo, after breakfast, we need to talk. You need to be aware of everything before you leave here. A lot of the other ranchers will be gathering again at the country store, and I need to go there for grain and other things. This time I would like for you to sit down at the table with me and hear what they say. We just had a town meeting. I will tell you the stories that were told there as we drive into town. Just keep in mind, though, that a lot of us have our own thoughts, and the question is this … are these stories fact or fiction?"

When it was daylight, I couldn't believe all the fog and clouds that hovered over the area. It looked like something out of an old Alfred Hitchcock movie. I needed to stay focused as I had a short time there, to try to find the remaining pieces of the puzzle that would hopefully fix this horrific secret that everyone here was living.

The drive into town was slow and scary. All the fog made it hard for my father to see the highway. When we did get to town, we went to the country store. Sitting there once again were some of the same people that congregated there each day. With everything that was going on, I didn't understand why they chose the store to go to, instead of staying in their own homes. Father explained that by them being there, they felt safer, and at the store they felt no fear as they were surrounded by numerous people. Everyone there would tell me their story, and I was to choose what I wanted to believe.

I hadn't shown Father the information I had brought with me, so I was fairly sure that most of what they talked about I would believe, considering the fact that at home I had copies of obituaries that were found in an old file cabinet in a research building in New York City. How out of the ordinary was that?

I wanted to wait until later in the day before I showed Father what I had to bring to the table. I was counting on the people there at that table to help me figure out the rest of what we would all be looking for.

When we sat down at the table, my father told everyone that it was okay if they wanted to share with me what they knew and had heard, or experienced, on Sleeping Indian Mountain.

The first one to speak was Ralph Winters. He said, "Years ago, Mylo, when you were in high school, there was a man named Peter Barnes who lived in a huge house below Sleeping Indian Mountain. Some of us believe that he was a doctor that could bring people who had passed away back to life by using black magic.

"None of us wanted anything to do with him, out of fear of what he was capable of. We would see his wife at different times in town, and she never spoke to any of us. It was like she always had a blank expression on her face. She was pale in complexion and her voice was different. There is no way I can explain it, other than she gave us the creeps.

"One day, an encyclopedia salesman came to town. He went door to door, trying to get all of us to buy them. None of us had told him to stay away from Peter's house, and what we believed Peter did there. When the salesman stopped at Peter's old house, he walked to the front door, convinced that Peter— having a nice big home— would have the money to buy a set of his encyclopedias from him.

"He knocked, and the door opened. The salesman couldn't see anyone standing there and kept saying, 'Hello? Hello?' After hesitating a short time on the front step, he entered the house. He continued to ask if anyone could hear him. By then, he was standing in the middle of the living room, thinking that he shouldn't be there.

"All of a sudden, the shutters on the window blew open. This startled the crap out of him. It was starting to rain and the wind blew hard. He knew he had to get out of there. When he turned to walk out of the house, he smelled an odor that was like decaying flesh. The smell got intense. By then, the salesman was so afraid that his mind told him to run and his legs couldn't move.

"Then he saw a group of people that had no color to their faces stumbling as they walked toward him, with their arms stretched out at him. He then started running in the opposite direction of what he believed to be a group of grotesque dead bodies. That was insane! How could they walk again?

"The terrified salesman ran all the way into town. Doug Pierce and I had gone there that day to get more barbed wire, and the salesman came running up to us, stuttering and shaking. The blood looked like it had drained from his face out of the fear that he had inside of him. I took the poor man home with me and listened to his story of what he believed he had seen. As he put it to me, 'The dead had walked again.'

"The next day, he didn't even want to go back to Peter's house to get his car. Before I took him to the bus station, we came back into town where the salesman told his story, here at this table, of how the people that were buried in the cemetery on Sleeping Indian Mountain had walked again. I told the salesman that we all believed that Peter was a doctor of science that used some form of black magic to awaken, or bring the dead back to life, but at that time the dead chose to stay on the mountain, where they killed and ate their prey."

Ralph had spoken, and no one said a word for a moment. Then Harry Albert started talking. "One evening, before it got dark, my wife and I were driving on the old road leading to the cemetery on the mountain, when thunder roared and the lightning lit up the sky. It began to hail and rain as if the sky had opened up. It got so bad, I couldn't see where I was driving on the road, as the windshield wipers couldn't keep up with the hail and rain pounding against them. Because of this, I slid partially off the side of the road into a shallow ditch. The only thing we could do was sit and wait until the storm quit.

"An hour went by with the downpour, and it was starting to get dark. Knowing all the stories of Sleeping Indian Mountain after dark, and the barriers that the county put across the road, along with the gate getting locked, I knew that I had to do whatever I needed to do, to get us out of there. I left the car and used my hands to dig out the mud that had formed around each tire. Even doing that, I wasn't sure it would be enough for me to be able to drive the car out of there.

"I looked again, and more mud was sliding down to keep each tire from moving. I threw myself to my knees, cupping my hands, and at times lying on the ground, removing the mud. I couldn't give up and worked faster. When I had cleared all the tires, I ran to the car and got the flowered wooden decorations that my wife and I were going to put beside the gravestones of our family and friends. The tires would need something scooted under each one that was solid and dry. After doing this, I returned to the car and told my wife that if it didn't work, we would be stuck there all night.

"I started the car and looked at my wife. All I could think about was getting us out of there and down off of Sleeping Indian. When I turned on the headlights, we saw a man stumbling and kind of leaning to his side with what appeared to be blood-stained clothes on, coming toward us. He was pale and had some blood dripping from his mouth. I threw the gear shift into drive and floored the foot pedal.

"As we drove out of there, mud and small, cracked boards were flying everywhere. I was driving right at this person and before I reached him, he stuck his arms out, as if to jerk me from the car. I drove past him, kicking up mud on him from the tires. When I could find a place to turn the car around again, I was going in his direction on the road to take us off the mountain. Expecting to see him either standing there or stumbling around on the road, I drove faster.

"When we got to the spot where he was, and we were, there was no sign of him. By then, my wife was crying from fear and I, too, just wanted to get as far away from the mountain as I could get. When we did reach the bottom of the mountain, and the end of the road on the mountain, there were men from the county department that were getting ready to close the gate. I went speeding through it. My wife and I haven't gone on Sleeping Indian since that night. That man up there *wasn't human!*"

As Father and I sat there, looking at each other and wondering who would speak next, an old man who had been sitting at the soda counter came over to the table and sat down. He said, "I, too, have a story I would like to tell that was told to me by my grandson.

"A while back, before the fog and clouds took over the town and the mountain, my grandson had been at a poker game with a few of his friends. They had gone there on their Harleys. They were going to spend the night in that house, so that they would be closer to town where the big Harley rally was taking place the next day.

"Later that evening, after poker, some of the riders decided they should add a new rule to their club. Every year from then on, including that night, there would be four of them that would be chosen by the group to make the ride to the top of Sleeping Indian. There they would place a flag with their names on it in the ground, to prove that they had done this. All four of them had heard stories and knew that Sleeping Indian Mountain had many secrets.

"Knowing this, they still wanted to make their club more daring and exciting. So, the four that were chosen rode their bikes to the barriers and gate. They cut the lock so that they could open it and ride up the mountain to plant their flag. As they started up the mountain road, they yelled, 'The Hog Rules!' By then, it was very dark ... and late. Some of the townspeople who lived below the mountain could hear the loud echo of the roaring Harleys as they rolled up the road, headed to the top of the mountain. If only they would have known at that moment that only three riders would return that night alive.

"When they reached their destination, they were feeling proud of themselves for defying everyone—the town, county laws and rules. They climbed off their bikes, laughing and bragging about what they had done. Then, one of the young men climbed back on his bike and rode it over to the perfect spot to plant the flag. The others also climbed on theirs and watched.

"Through the trees, with the still of the mountain at that time, three of the men who were watching the fourth man plant the flag could hear the rustling of the tree branches and the wind starting to blow. They sensed that they weren't alone. The three riders yelled at the other rider to leave and follow them off of the mountain, as they weren't alone.

"The young man sat on his bike with a beer can raised to toast all of them. When the three that were yelling for him to leave saw images of something coming through the trees at him, they left. The young man was so proud of himself that he had planted the flag, he just kept drinking his beer as he sat on his bike. Since it was still running, he couldn't hear what the others had said to him. The other three turned their bikes around, and a little ways down the road, they stopped to look back, to see if their friend had made it out of there safe. Instead, he had met his fate. All they could hear was him screaming. They saw the images—who they thought were people—standing over him with blood that had splattered everywhere.

"By the time they left, their friend had stopped screaming. He was dead. They rode back without their friend and their club flag, only to find the sheriff and deputies waiting at the bottom of the mountain road. Shaken and still upset at what they had witnessed, the young men told their story. They had survived Sleeping Indian, but their friend didn't. Out of fear, the sheriff and his men refused to go on the mountain.

"Shortly after, the fog got worse and the clouds. As far as I know, the young man who lost his life that night is still lying up there next to his flag, covered in blood. One of the riders is my grandson. He told me the story when I went to visit him at Fairview Mental Hospital. That night destroyed a lot of lives."

The old man got up from his chair and walked out the door.

"Who is that man, Father?" I asked.

"He is our mayor, Mylo. John Relms. I called him before we left this morning, and asked him to join us at the table, to tell you his story," Father replied.

Next to speak was Mike Baker.

"Mylo, a few months ago, I went hiking up the mountain. I, too, knew the danger that I was in, but because I am the editor for our newspaper here, I wanted to take some pictures from Sleeping Indian, to send with a write-up to a famous magazine company, showing beautiful pictures of our town. It was getting harder to come up here, and I wanted good pictures before the Governor declared it a disaster area and everyone was banned from the mountain. I parked my car off the mountain road and hiked up the mountain.

"As I was hiking through the trees, I saw a

huge metal box that was placed on the ground. Then, as I kept hiking, I found another one. There might have been more, but not knowing what it was, who put it there or why, I chose to leave them alone. At that time, I thought about taking pictures of them, but decided that if the government had put them there, that it would be better for me to keep this to myself. Each one of them weren't far from the old cemetery. I saw what appeared to be smoke coming from them, but could see that there was no fire.

"After a short time, what I believed to be smoke turned into thick fog and was getting worse. There was no way I could take pictures, so I started back down the mountainside. Passing the boxes, I was convinced the government had something to do with this and they were doing an experiment or research up there that we weren't supposed to know about. Otherwise, why was this happening?

"In an hour or two it would be dark, and I, too, had to find my car and get off the mountain. As I walked down the trails, I could hear not just the twigs on the ground that I was breaking as I walked along, and the bushes moving from me. I was not alone, as I could hear other bushes rustling in the wind and other twigs snapping. I wanted to believe that I was hearing a bear or a mountain lion that had picked up my scent. Whatever it was, I had to walk faster.

"When I got closer to the road and my car, my boot lace caught on a tree limb that had fallen over.

I turned around to see if whatever was stalking me would show itself. It turned into *them*.

"I saw many people that were coming my way, bumping into each other as they stumbled down the mountainside. Their arms were stretched out. They could only walk slowly and this was an advantage that I had. Taking out my knife, I cut the boot lace to free my boot. I finished running down the trail and to my car. As I drove away, in my mirror, I could still see them coming to the road.

"We all have so many questions as to who these people are. Why they are dangerous, and why do they look the way they do? What caused this, as we all know the dead can't walk, or can they?"

Mike Baker was finished and my previous boss, Megan, sat down in the chair next to me. She wanted to share her story with me.

"Before spring, during the end of winter, I had gone outside to get some firewood. After building the fire, I turned around and saw a pale-faced young woman looking at me through the glass on the window. She had a blank look and her nails were at least ten inches long. She put her hands on the glass and ran her nails down it. I tried screaming, but nothing came out.

"I then ran upstairs to get my husband. Before we reached the living room, the woman had left. After explaining this woman's pale complexion to my husband, we agreed that maybe she was cold and needed shelter. Maybe that was why her face was so white. The next morning, when it was light enough outside, both my husband and I went out to see if the woman had spent the night in the barn.

"We never found her, but we did find many footprints in the snow. The woman's print and the others, as she was not alone, showed six toes and no shoe print. It was freezing outside. Who all was there had ripped our chickens apart. There were blood and feathers everywhere.

"I remember, Mylo, when you worked here on your last day, wishing you wouldn't leave, but with all that is happening in Applegrove and the other areas, I wanted you to be safe. This is definitely not the right place for you."

Megan smiled, hugged me, and walked away from the table. The only person at the table who hadn't talked was my father. He proceeded to tell me about the night he found Rocky, and the graphics of what he and Mother had seen.

Father said, "We didn't know whether to tell you about everything we had seen that night, Mylo. You were only 16. We were afraid that if you knew, you would either be so afraid, you wouldn't want to leave the house, or you would be my curious little Mylo and try to solve all the mysteries by yourself. The rules of our home did become firmer, and there were days when you didn't see me, but I was watching and there if you needed protection.

"As you got older, the sightings of these people and the stories grew. When you left here for the city, your mother and I believed that all of this would stop and the National Guard would be able to discover the secret. The fog got worse all over the mountain and has drifted into this town and the surrounding areas as well. We haven't seen the sun in months for all the cloud coverage as well."

Father told me his story and I told him that I understood why they, at that time, didn't tell me everything. I would have gone looking for something before I'd thought it out first.

Now, with all the stories of several reputable people, I was convinced that Doctor Terry Belmar and his father, Wayne, planted the huge boxes on the mountain. Adam mentioned that day, when he snuck into the lab, how he had seen a huge metal box sitting there.

The copies of the obituary pages being tucked away and hidden in a cabinet were associated with death, and Ralph Winters referred to the salesman telling him that the dead were walking again. Also, the man believed to be a doctor of science that perhaps used black magic to raise the dead.

So much was said today that made me wonder if Peter knew Doctor Terry Belmar and Doctor Wayne Belmar.

Again, with all that I heard and what my father had told me, I knew that what Father told me was true. I had to determine what was fact or fiction, and to choose what I believed.

19

Could This Change the World?

Father and I thanked everyone at the table for their stories. We left the country store and were on our way back home. On the drive back, Father and I discussed all of it and, because my mother and father had seen grotesque people eating the neck of my horse, I had to believe that these people did exist. As for the dead being able to dig their way out of a grave, with tons of dirt on top of it, and walk again was something I wasn't sure was possible. It truly was insane. As far as I knew, it wasn't possible.

But then again, why were there copies of obituary papers from so many people who had passed away, sitting in an old file cabinet in New York City, miles away from here?

At last, Father and I made our way back to the house. Now was the time that I needed to talk to him, and with his help maybe we could figure out the last piece of missing information that we needed. Mother sat down with us to hear what I had to talk about.

"Father, I have something to show you, but first I need to speak to you and Mother about things of importance to me."

"We are listening, Mylo."

"As you already know, all three of the doctors were stunned to learn when I was hired that I came from Applegrove. At that time, Doctor Terry Belmar hired someone to follow me throughout the Wayne Belmar Research Industries building. He was doing this mainly, I believe, because Doctor Phillips and Doctor Neil didn't trust me. All of them were afraid that I would hear something, or find something that would cause a problem for their lives or careers.

"I could tell that I was being followed as the same man was waiting for me every morning in the lobby to go to the same elevator and floor that my office room is on, and the hallways that lead to every room in the building. There were times when I would overhear a conversation between all three doctors talking about how their research was going to change the world, and everyone would know that they were the scientists who did this.

"A week ago, I managed to outwalk the man who was following me. A person pushing a cart had gotten in front of him as he was following me. He was stuck there for a while, and so I took the stairs to get away from him. On my floor, I ducked into a room where I stood and barely looked out of it, to wait until the man had walked by, looking for me. When Doctor Phillips saw him frantically looking for me, he was so upset, he fired my stalker, and then he talked to Doctor Belmar about it.

"Of course, Doctor Neil and Doctor Phillips were concerned that I would be on my own in the building, but Doctor Belmar told them that they might be overreacting as his son, Adam, had been keeping me busy.

"Doctor Phillips, in a conversation, said he would stop things with me if he needed to. At that moment, I knew that this man was capable of anything. I had called and spoken to you and Mother. You had confirmed that Doctor Terry Belmar and his father, Doctor Wayne Belmar, were involved in research on Sleeping Indian.

"With all the bits and pieces that I had already put together, I decided to talk to Adam. He told me how secretive his father and grandfather were with their research years ago. Also, how he was left alone in his father's office. After a while, he went looking for him. He found his father and grandfather in a lab, where he saw a big metal box. It had something coming out of it. When he tried to sneak out, he got caught. His father told him that he was never to reveal anything he had seen or heard that day to anyone ... ever.

"Soon after, the lab doors were made stronger and the locks now consist of a code before they will open. Remember when Mike Baker said he had found a couple of huge boxes while hiking, and that fog started coming out, and how there could have been more of them? These boxes that he was speaking about had to have come from the lab.

"I wonder if Doctor Terry and Doctor Wayne Belmar knew Peter, the man who was believed to be practicing black magic, to make it so that the dead buried on the mountain could walk again. With what I heard in the city, I knew that I had to try to find more clues to help Adam learn the truth about his father, grandfather, Doctor Neil's and Doctor Phillips' research.

"Through the answers, there may be a way to solve the secrets of Sleeping Indian Mountain. I want all of you to be safe here again and be able to lead normal lives. I also was able to have a spare key made at work for an old file cabinet. One day, I saw Doctor Phillips stashing a paper in it. He was looking around, to make sure he didn't get seen, and when I entered the office room, he looked surprised. That is when I had a locksmith make a key for me. Inside, I found copies of obituaries of many people who passed away many years ago. Some of them were more current. There were not only obituary pages of people who had passed away in the city, but also in Applegrove. I have been wondering why they would secretly have them and keep them in an old file cabinet. Also, what use are these papers to them?

"I believe they saved the old keys from the lab doors before all of that was changed. They, too, were in there. I found a small trap door and in it was a copy of Doctor Wayne Belmar's obituary. It was carefully folded and put in there. I have a suspicion that Doctor Phillips is hiding that paper from Doctor Belmar and maybe Doctor Neil."

My father and mother sat there, hanging on every word that I said. By then, I had gotten the copies of the obituaries for Father to look at. "Do you recognize anyone?" I asked as Father and Mother looked through them.

"Yes, I do," Father replied.

"What do you think about all of this?" I asked.

"Mylo, as far as the copies go, I will need to give it some thought, along with everything else you have told us. As for the story you told, it sounds like you have been taking too many chances at work to gather this information. You will always be my curious little Mylo. The research you did is very convincing.

"Maybe I, too, can do a little research of my own here. I know it is pointless for me to tell you that you can't go back to the city. I think that you have grown very attached to Adam Belmar. This man must be very special to you. I think you should include him in all of this now, as apparently you trust him. He needs to know this. I want you to be careful and stop taking chances." Father was very adamant about what he had to say.

"All right, I will include Adam in on what I know, and see if he can fill in the blanks."

"It sounds like maybe Doctor Terry Belmar and Doctor Wayne Belmar might have known the so-called doctor of science. I am speaking about Peter Barnes. What they created is, or could, change the world in a *bad* way. If whatever is happening here reaches out to other towns and cities, we could all be fighting for our lives all over the world. It sounds to me like, with the exception of Adam, all the other doctors are mad scientists."

20

Too Many Secrets

Morning came and again I had to say goodbye to my parents. With everything that was going on in Applegrove, the city and at Wayne Belmar Research Industries, it was going to be a solemn day for me. I knew that Mother and Father would also find it tough to see me leave.

I felt so close to finding the finished pieces of the complicated puzzle that I had no choice but to keep going. There were too many lives at stake to quit now. Two of those lives were very precious to me.

Again, as I entered the kitchen, I saw Father hunched over in his chair with his rifle across his lap and his hand on it. This had to end!

Father woke up and stretched his back. He looked into my eyes. I know he could see that I was determined to help everyone. When I looked into his eyes, I saw worry and tiredness. I could have stayed in the city until I had all the answers, but I needed to be here to see them and add answers to what I already had.

Father was insistent on my sharing everything with Adam and I would find the right moment to do this.

My father, being the smart man that he is and knowing now as much as I did, would try to figure all this out, unless Adam and I could figure it out first.

Once again it was a quick goodbye, and I was backing the rental car out of the garage. Waving and throwing kisses my parents' way, it was time to fight the fog and the low clouds in the area.

Today it was a longer ride back to the airport to catch my flight before I could see a blue sky. The fog and clouds were spreading to other towns. All of this insanity that came from Doctor Belmar and his father would need to stop now before it spread.

The trip back to the city was long. All I could think about was what I had heard, found out and knew. In fact, the flight attendant came to me and said, "You need to fasten your seatbelt. We will be landing soon at JFK."

I nodded and did as she said. In the parking lot was my own car waiting to take me to my hotel.

I called Adam and he was on his way to talk with me. He had given his father the human brains that were now functioning the way they should be. He was finished with his research. Now I needed his help with mine.

There was a soft knock on the door. Adam arrived and, with that, I was greeted with a long, soft hug. He had missed me, as a part of me did him.

"Mylo, I am so happy to see you. I was afraid you wouldn't come back."

"I had two reasons for coming back, Adam. You ...

and the reason why I needed to go home right now."

"I'm ecstatic, but confused."

"When I am finished talking today, you will understand." I started telling him everything from what he had seen in his father's and grandfather's lab when he was a boy, to how I had gotten rid of the stalker in the building, and what I overheard with all the other doctors, and the way Doctor Phillips was looking around before I entered my office room while putting a page of an obituary into the old file cabinet.

I told him how I pretended to be a scientist who had lost the key to the file cabinet and had a locksmith come to make another one for me. I told him about the obituary pages I found in there and how uncanny it was to not only see ones from the city, but also from Applegrove. I mentioned the old keys to the labs that were buried under the obituary pages, and how a copy of his grandfather's obituary had been folded and slipped into a secret compartment.

I told Adam the fact that my father had solid proof that his father and grandfather had been in Applegrove, researching the mountain years ago. All the stories I had heard from several people in Applegrove's country store—all respected for the character they possess—what my father had said, how he was going to do his own research there.

When I finished talking, I had a question for Adam. "One of the obituary pages was Amy Belmar, Adam. Some of the page looked like it had faded with age. Do you know this woman?" I asked.

Stepping forward with a solemn face and then turning his back to me, Adam replied, "Yes, that is the name of my mother. She was killed when I was very young. I was too young to remember her. As she was riding the subway, a man with a gun, who was trying to rob people, shot her in the head. He wanted her money and her wedding ring. She gave him all her money, but refused to give him her wedding ring. After he shot her, the subway came to an abrupt stop. The man fell forward and some of the men jumped him, got the gun, and held him there until the police arrived.

"My father had a write-up put in the paper, but told me that he was taking my mother to her favorite place in the world to be buried. First, he said that he would keep her at the morgue because he had something he needed to do first with Grandfather. My father and mother were very close. I'll never forget the sadness in his eyes. After that, my father changed. He hired a live-in nanny to take care of me, and spent many hours at the lab with Grandfather. I hardly saw him.

"That day, when I got caught in the lab, I had gone in there because I wanted to find him and spend time with him. Months passed, and I was told that the research they were doing would benefit us someday. Not long after that, he told me that Grandfather and himself were going to be gone for a while. Also, to be good for the nanny. He was gone for weeks. Even the nanny didn't know where they went. If she knew, she never told me. There was a secret that I was never to find out about, and finally maybe I will."

Adam turned around to look at me. I saw a tear drop from his eye. He rubbed the tear away and asked, "What is the other question, Mylo?"

"First, I need to say that I am sorry for what happened to your mother. That had to be very hard for you, and your father back then. Sometimes losing someone we love does strange things to us.

"However, what is happening in Applegrove has, and is, affecting many people. It has been proven that your father and grandfather were there. After they left Sleeping Indian Mountain, the fog started and the low clouds set in. This started when I, too, was very young, but only got worse as I grew older.

"Now it is terrible all over the area. With all the information that I have, I am sure that your father and grandfather caused this bizarre behavior. It's like the awakening of the unknown. Can I count on you to help me find the secrets of Sleeping Indian Mountain, no matter what the outcome reveals?"

Without hesitation, Adam said, "Yes, Mylo. There have been too many secrets for years. Many lives are in danger and have been destroyed. If my father is the one who created this with my grandfather, then this won't go away until Father stops it.

"Thinking back, Shawn Phillips and Ann Neil were both working in Switzerland when my mother was killed. Not long after that, Grandfather hired them to work for him. Yes, Mylo, I will help you. But this could take a while longer, as I can't confront my father straight out with anything right now, as I know that he won't be honest with me. We need some more information first."

"I know. I will follow your lead now," I replied.

Everything was out in the open now, and again it could turn into a waiting game, but not for long.

Until Adam left, we spent the evening sitting on the couch, holding each other and talking about other things. I wanted to smile, laugh and take our minds in a different direction.

21

What Was Created

Monday morning and back to work again. None of the three doctors knew or suspected anything about my leaving the city to go back home for a short visit.

As usual, I walked through the building and to my office room, wearing a smile. I wanted everyone there to believe that I was extremely happy to be working there.

Coming out of his office was Doctor Phillips. No smile and again no "Good morning, Malon."

All he said was, "When Doctor Neil gets here, tell her to come into my office."

"Okay, Doctor Phillips," I said as he shut his office door. My imagination took off again. I was wondering if maybe I didn't get everything back into the old file cabinet and Doctor Phillips was getting ready to tell Doctor Neil about it.

Within a few minutes, Doctor Neil came into my office room door. I told her that Doctor Phillips was expecting her and to go on into his office.

After she shut the door, I couldn't hear them. Expecting the worst, I sat at my desk, waiting for the outcome. Whatever was said in there was short, as Doctor Neil came back out and left my office room. I could breathe again. I knew that if Doctor Phillips had suspected anything, they both would have come out together to confront me.

After a while, I was given papers that made absolutely no sense to me to type and entered them into his personal office computer. These were no different, just different numbers than the last ones that he'd handed to me to take care of.

Today there would be no snooping, as Adam and my father were going to try to find the last bit of information needed. A part of me felt relieved. I knew I could trust Adam to take care of it on this end and my father in Applegrove.

In Doctor Belmar's lab, Doctor Phillips and Doctor Neil walked in to discuss something with Doctor Belmar.

"I have been waiting for both of you," Doctor Belmar said as he took his surgical gloves off.

"We're here, Terry. We are somewhat skeptical on Adam's finished results," Doctor Phillips replied.

"What do you have to say, Ann? Do you have any doubts? Once the human brains are put in place, there is no turning back. We have spent twenty years working toward this moment. Now we are ready for it. If things go well, we will be on our way to success, and to Applegrove with a new specimen. The specimens that are there will be brought back here for correction," Doctor Belmar said with an encouraged look on his face.

"This all sounds good, Terry, but don't you think we should try it here in the city first?" Ann asked.

"The specimen that we have been working on is from here. This will be our first test. It might take a couple of days to take effect. This will mean twenty-four hours watch with all three of us taking turns. A brain from many that Adam worked on and reconstructed that appears to be working is here right now, and ready. Instead of talking about it, I am ready to just do it. I believe in my son's work. I know it will work." Doctor Belmar had spoken and was getting impatient with Doctor Phillips and Doctor Neil. He pulled his surgical gloves back on and they took the sheet off of the specimen. Work was in progress in the lab.

Back home in Applegrove, my father had decided to do a little investigating of his own. He had gone into town to the country store. He was asking a lot of the men who were sitting around the table, telling stories about Sleeping Indian Mountain, to join him on the search up the mountain. By doing this, they would catch or destroy these people that everyone believed had been awakened with black magic.

Everyone my father spoke with agreed that they'd had enough and were tired of waiting for the National Guard to land on top of the mountain to stop the bizarre unknown. The plan was in effect, and all of them agreed that they would go to every business that had rifles, handguns and other weapons. Every man would load all of them. Early in the morning, they would gather at the store with what they had to take up there.

There were many caves and openings in the huge rocks, where they could take shelter or maybe hide, if need be. If everyone waited much longer, time would run out. This time there would be no vehicles on the mountain. Whatever these things were, they had to be watched, and a vehicle made too much noise.

As Father told the men about his plan in the store, he added, "This is the only way we can destroy them. We will be able to see them better, walking."

My father and the other men were taking a big chance not knowing what all of them were about to face and discover. There was more to it than they knew, and destroying a few wasn't the solution. Only Doctor Belmar, Doctor Phillips and Doctor Neil knew the way to stop it, and the truth was about to come out. This horrific secret would unfold before the end of the week.

At the time, I didn't know this, or that I would be back in Applegrove standing on top of Sleeping Indian Mountain once more.

The day at work was over, and it was time for me to go home. Adam and I had decided that our time at work together would be sparing, as we didn't know what the doctors, including his own father, were capable of. There was too much at stake now.

Adam said that Doctor Phillips and Doctor Neil would not only be suspicious of me, but also him if they were seen together too much at work. Everything had to run smoothly. My life might be in danger.

When I returned to my room at the hotel, I saw the light on my phone's answering machine blinking. I had a message.

"Mylo, it's your father. I just wanted to let you know that first thing in the morning, myself—along with all the capable men in the area—are going to start preparing to make our way up Sleeping Indian Mountain. We have lost so much and can't wait for the National Guard to get here. The fog and low clouds are even worse than when you were here. It is spreading toward surrounding towns, and before long, whatever these people are, they will destroy us. We have to find a way to destroy them. Don't worry. Your mother will be safe while I am gone. I hope you told Adam about his father and grandfather. Right now, I'm not sure what they created. With all of us working together, maybe we can stop this insanity. Be careful, and let Adam deal with this now. I love you, Mylo. Talk soon."

After hearing this message, I wasn't sure how to react. I agreed with Father on all the men in town tracking these things, for a change. My family and the townspeople had been the victims and prey for years. Then again, my father and the other men were walking into the unknown, and this is what scared me. If Adam didn't have answers in a few days, or my father, I would be returning to the mountain to stand alongside my father and the other men. I had an advantage that they didn't.

With all the adventures that Rocky and I had made on Sleeping Indian, I had found more than just caves and holes in the rocks to hide. There were even safe spots hidden in the ground where they wouldn't be seen.

I had heard enough for the day, but called Adam anyway. I was told that he was on his way over to his father's house to speak to him. Adam said he was going to choose his words very carefully with him, and would find out something that would help us before he left the house.

This was good enough for me. We would make progress. Another day ended for me.

22

Owner of Cemetery

As I was sleeping, Adam did go see his father. The butler let Adam in when the doorbell rang.

"Good evening, Master Adam."

"Good evening, Rockford. Is my father available for visitors?"

"I will tell him you are here."

Doctor Belmar had heard the doorbell. He came down the stairs to see who his visitor was. Adam had told me once that when his mother was alive, she was the one who answered the door, cooked, cleaned and took care of his father and himself. Also, how much he missed her and the simpler times before things changed with Doctor Belmar after his mother was killed.

Seeing Adam that late in the evening was a surprise to Doctor Belmar. "Adam, my son, what brings you by this time of night?"

"Not much, Father. I was thinking today about how we hardly talk outside of work anymore. I would like to change that."

"You are right, son. Come into my den. I was looking earlier at some old photos of your mother, and thinking about how nice it would be to have her with us. Let me show some pictures to you."

They walked into the den. Adam noticed that his father's eyes looked wild. With every year that had passed, it seemed to Adam that his father was sinking more and more into the past, but because of the secret he was carrying, he was trying to change the future.

With his father's eyes still strained, wild and crazy, Adam and Doctor Belmar sat down in the den. Doctor Belmar reached into his desk and pulled out many photos of his deceased wife, Amy. With the photos of her were pictures of all three of them together. Some of them were taken days before her death. This woman was his world, along with Adam.

Adam asked, "Father, can we talk? I love looking at the old photos, but Mother is gone. We can't bring her back."

"Adam, your mother is not gone. You will see her again very soon."

At that moment, Adam questioned what his father said. "What do you mean by soon, Father?"

"Oh, you know, Adam. She will return someday."

Adam could tell that his father was slowly passing into another world as he was talking in circles, and his eyes still looked wild. It was time to change the subject. How little did Adam know that his father had given him a clue.

"Tell me, Father, did the brain that was on ice work the way you wanted it to today?"

"The brain? Oh, the brain! Shawn and Ann will help me with that tomorrow, Adam. From what I could see, you did a fine job. It looked like it was back to functioning order again. If it works as good as it appears to look, Shawn, Ann and I will be leaving the city for a while. There is something out there that I need to change that has gone bad."

"Can I, too, be included in this project, Father?"

"No, Adam. I will need you to stay here and handle other projects and research while we are gone. Besides, Malon would miss you," his father said as he chuckled.

"Okay, Father. Malon and I are just friends. Nothing more. Occasionally we have dinner together." Adam was trying to make it look as though he and I were not romantically involved, to throw his father in a different direction than how he and I really felt about one another.

Adam had something that he had found out to contribute to what I had. He was done talking to his father for the night. He got up from his chair in the den and told Doctor Belmar that he should probably leave. When he turned around, he asked, "Where did you bury Mother?"

With a question that he hadn't heard from Adam in many years as Adam grew into a man, Doctor Belmar replied, "Your grandfather and I buried her in a small town away from the city. That was her favorite place."

"Will we ever go visit her grave, Father?"

"Yes, Adam. You will see your mother again."

With that being said, Adam turned back around again and walked out of the den. He said goodbye to Rockford and left the house.

Adam was sure that his father was even more sick than he realized. He wanted all the secrets that his father harbored to surface, but he also wanted his father well again. For the next few days, he planned on spending a lot of time with him or, at least, what Doctor Terry Belmar would allow.

Morning came. I had just slipped on my heels and grabbed my jacket. As I walked toward the door to leave, the phone rang. It was Adam.

"Good morning."

"Good morning, Mylo."

"Did you visit your father last night?"

"Yes. I didn't stay long, but I did get some more answers. Father mentioned that my mother was buried in a small town that she always loved. He also said we would see her soon ... if the research I have been working on turns out to be as good as it looks. At that time, he, Shawn and Ann are leaving the city for a while, to fix a project that went bad. We now have proof that Applegrove is where my father and grandfather did research on the mountain.

"My father would have told me the name of the town if you and I hadn't met. In fact, he brought up that you and I are together now. I told him we are just casual friends. Shortly after I arrived there, we were looking through old photos of Mother. Also ones taken of her, Father and I. He thinks the research he is working on will change the world.

"Mylo, call your father and ask him to contact the cemetery's funeral home. I need to make sure that my mother was buried on the mountain. I will cover for you at work, to give you a little extra time."

"Okay. I can call my father now. I know that Doctor Phillips will have more pages for me to type. I have no clue what they are, so after he leaves, I will make copies. Maybe after work you can stop by here and tell me what they mean."

"Yes, I will look at them. I will tell Shawn that you had to take the train into work. Shawn will understand that, as he knows that the train is never on time at its scheduled stops. He won't scold you when you get there."

"Okay, Adam. We will talk tonight."

"Okay."

I hung up and immediately called my father. Since the time difference EST was two hours ahead of MST, I was fairly sure that I would still find him at home before he left to go into town.

The phone rang twice and I heard, "Mylo, I see you got my message."

"I did. I have some other news for you. Last night, Adam went to see his father. Doctor Belmar told Adam that his mother is buried in a small town that she loved. Also that he and Adam himself will see her soon. It sounds like Doctor Belmar is crazier than before, when he and his father went to Sleeping Indian Mountain. Adam asked me if you could find out at the funeral home if his mother is buried there. This is very important with this mystery that we are trying to solve. Please let me know soon, Father, because by the end of the week, we should have all the answers we need to put an end to the secrets of Sleeping Indian Mountain."

"I will go check when I get to town, Mylo. If it is true, we might wait a day or two before going up on the mountain. If the secrets can all fall into place, maybe Doctor Belmar himself can stop it."

"Maybe? Adam said his father liked the work that he had done with his research. That has something to do with the research for the project that Doctor Terry Belmar and Doctor Wayne Belmar did many years ago. If things go well in the lab, Doctor Belmar, Doctor Phillips and Doctor Neil will be leaving the city to supposedly fix what went bad in an area. That would mean Adam's father's return to the mountain with the other two doctors. Hopefully, you can postpone the walk up the mountain for now, to buy us more time."

"I think I can do this as long as the information about Adam's mother is correct. I will call you tonight."

"Okay, Father."

I had done what Adam asked and was leaving my hotel room to go to work. Today I would take the train. I couldn't afford for Doctor Phillips to catch me in a lie.

It took quite a while with all the stops, to get to where I needed to be, but with the walk, I was finally at my office room. Adam had talked to Doctor Phillips. He had cleared it for me to be late. When I sat down at my desk, there were more papers for me to type and enter into the office computer.

Today I made some copies for Adam to look at tonight, when he came to see me after we had both stopped working for the day. I had the opportunity to complete this before Doctor Phillips came back to his office.

In Applegrove, my father had gone to town. He was anxious to talk to the man that owned the mortuary and cemetery on Sleeping Indian Mountain. After sifting through old records, the owner did confirm that Amy Belmar had been buried at the old cemetery on the mountain. There was something else that had been said that made the hair stand up on the back of my father's neck.

"Years ago, before the fog got thick, I went up on the mountain to make sure that my worker had cut the grass and cleaned away all the broken branches from around the tombstones," the man told Father. "This was after Amy Belmar's husband and another man came to me, wanting to buy a burial plot. I was told that if I would have my worker prepare the plot for burial, that both of them would bury Amy Belmar themselves. So I agreed, and I sent my worker up on Sleeping Indian to dig the hole and put the tombstone in place. My helper did his job and left, planning to return later to cover the hole and plant grass around the area.

"Later on, when he did return, he saw Amy's husband and the other man carrying what appeared to be a metal box. When my worker confronted Mr.

Belmar with this, he was told that they were doing research up there as well as him burying his wife. The hole was covered and my helper left. He believed that both men had covered the hole themselves.

"When I went up there months later, the tombstones were in place. The grass and dirt had been dug up. The caskets were open. Some were empty. At the time, I reported it to the authorities as being caused from grave robbers looking for jewelry that had been buried with the bodies. Also, that wild animals were eating bodies in the caskets. I covered the caskets, empty or not, with dirt as I didn't need bad publicity, or the animals to eat any more from the bodies that were there. The ones whose resting ground had been disturbed were those of people who had been recently buried. This was not talked about, because of what I believed would just frighten everyone who wanted to bury their loved ones in the cemetery.

"After the men that were doing research left town is when many low clouds started forming and the fog. The community of Applegrove always respected the old cemetery. As for the metal boxes, I looked around some, to see what my worker was talking about. I saw nothing and assumed that whatever it was had been put back in the big trailer that Amy Belmar's husband and the other man had taken up on top of the mountain."

The man had told his story to Father. After Father left, he was even more intrigued and didn't buy the assumption of a grave robber wanting jewelry. There was much more going on than that happening.

From there, Father went to the store to meet with the men who had gathered together to start their journey walking up the mountain. Today, Father had several stories to tell them. They needed to know everything he knew.

For that day, at least, the trip up the mountain wouldn't happen. For them, this would give us a few more days that we needed.

In Doctor Belmar's lab, Doctor Phillips and Doctor Neil had worked with Doctor Belmar to complete the project that they had been working on for twenty years.

"It looks good, Terry," Doctor Phillips said as he walked across the room.

"I told you that Adam would handle this," Doctor Belmar replied.

"It really is too soon to tell. After a few days, we should know for sure," Doctor Neil said as she pulled her surgical cap off.

"Starting now, we are taking turns in here to take notes, monitoring the meters and watching the activity on the lab computer," Doctor Belmar instructed.

"Okay, Terry. If it is all right with you and Ann, I would like to take my turn last. In my office, I am monitoring the charges of energy, to see if the increase is still in effect on Sleeping Indian. If it is, we should be able to sneak in and sneak out without being seen. While we are there, we can also make sure of the slight electrical charge in the air. We won't need any of that if this goes well," Doctor Phillips replied.

"I will take my turn first," said Ann. "Also I will measure all the activity in here. Since this is the first day, I am asking you to please keep your pagers turned on. I might need help."

"This works for both of you," Terry said. "Be prepared to leave here in a few days. We will be gone for a while. Shawn, tomorrow I will need you to bring me a report on the electrical activity, and also on the functioning of the thick fog and clouds."

Not knowing what they had done in the lab that day, I took my copy of a paper that I had typed into Doctor Phillips' office computer home with me and waited for a call from my father.

When he did call, he explained what the cemetery owner had said. I was relieved that he had found Amy Belmar. Also, I was relieved that Father wouldn't be on the mountain tonight.

Later, I was hoping to hear from Adam.

23

Peter? Who's Peter?

I made it to work on time the next day. Adam must have been looking for his father as I never heard from him the night before.

Doctor Phillips came out of his office and told me, "I see you made it to work on time today, Malon. Today I am letting you leave early. I have work to do in here and nothing that concerns you."

I still had the copies of the papers that I had entered into the computer the day before, so I sat down at my desk and did the work that was waiting for me for that day. Doctor Phillips had hung up his lab coat. I could see that he was there in his office for a while, if not the whole day.

Nothing for me to do next, but enter the information from the new papers into the office computer, and then leave to go home.

That evening as I waited for Adam to arrive, I kept going over all the stories I had heard from the townspeople from Applegrove. I heard a knock on the door. It was Adam juggling a box of pizza and drinks for us. I couldn't help but laugh at him when I opened the door and saw him.

"Let me help you, Adam," I said as I took the drink carrier.

"Thanks, Mylo. I really did need your help. There was a couple who were ready to enter the elevator when I was, but because of my clumsiness, juggling—and the fear of wearing the pizza—and the drinks—they changed their minds on taking the elevator with me. I tried not to laugh when they walked away, but couldn't stop myself."

"That is funny, Adam," I replied. I loved the effort that Adam always put into helping me, or trying to make things better and easier for me.

After we ate, it was time to get serious. I walked to the counter to get the copies I had made of the information that Doctor Phillips had me enter into his office computer every day.

Adam studied the copies and said, "Mylo, this is some kind of code, or Shawn is measuring an electrical apparatus to get some readings. This looks like readings from an electromagnetic field. Do you get papers every day that are similar to these?"

"Yes. Every day I enter them into Doctor Phillips' office computer."

"I am going to take the copies with me and see if I can hack into his computer. After I figure this out, I will destroy all the papers that you have given me. Don't worry, Mylo. I won't let anything happen to you."

Adam put his arms around me and pulled me close to him. It felt very good to feel the way I did. For the first time in my life, I felt as if I was falling in love. He continued to hold me until he had to leave. His next stop would be his father's house once again.

I knew in my heart that with all the secrets that Doctor Terry Belmar had kept from Adam for twenty years, about what he and his father had done on Sleeping Indian Mountain, Adam was hoping that he could bring his father back to reality.

But from what I had been told, I knew it was too late. I could see that Doctor Belmar wasn't going to change. I filled Adam in on everything my father had told me. At last he knew where his mother was buried.

There was no turning back, or changing what had happened in the past, but maybe there would be a chance for the future. Before Adam left my hotel room, he told me he would talk to me again tomorrow night after work.

At Doctor Belmar's house, Adam was met by Rockford at the door. Adam asked again if his father was home, and was told that he was in his den. Adam told him that he would show himself to the den.

Sitting in his chair at his desk was Doctor Belmar with his back to the door. He didn't hear Adam come into the room. Before Adam had a chance to announce himself to his father, he overheard him talking to an old photo of his mother.

"Amy, it won't be long now. Everything will be like it was before. What I did years ago didn't work the way it was supposed to. This time it did. Peter promised me when Father and I were there, that with what we had done, everything would be okay with his help. He lied to us and things went bad. Peter got scared and left. I can't find him."

Before Doctor Belmar could say anything else, his pager sounded. He got up from his desk and saw Adam standing there. "Oh, Adam, I didn't expect to see you again so soon. I need to call Ann."

He left the den to call Doctor Neil without Adam hearing their conversation. This was what he had done since Adam was a young boy, after his mother was killed.

While waiting, Adam tried to figure out what his father had been saying as he had talked to that photo. How could things ever be like they were before? Mother was deceased and buried in a cemetery. Why did he think that he could justify what he and Grandfather did many years ago? All it did was hurt innocent people. How did he think that he would be able to change the world, and work now as it was supposed to years ago? Who was Peter? How did he fit into this mess they had created?

Adam, like me, was trying to put the pieces of the puzzle together that we were looking for. Doctor Belmar had gone to a room where he couldn't be heard, to speak to Doctor Neil. This way neither Adam, nor Rockford, could hear his words in the conversation.

"Ann, is there something wrong?"

"No, Terry, on the contrary. The activity in here is going very well. In fact, there is a feeling of a small electrical charge in the air. I just wanted to let you know. I will be packed and ready to go in a few days as planned, if this continues to go well."

"Ann, I'm glad you gave me an update. I will take over tomorrow. I am checking results with Shawn before I come to the lab."

"See you tomorrow," Ann replied.

When Doctor Belmar returned to Adam, he was telling him how he really needed to call it a day and go to bed. Also, that he would be working in the lab all day tomorrow, and the entire night. Then he excused himself and left his den.

Because of all this strange behavior, Adam knew that it was just a matter of days before this secret his father had been carrying would be known by everyone involved.

As Adam got ready to leave the house, he saw Rockford waiting in the living room, ready to let him out of the house, so he could bolt the front door. This was extremely strange to Adam, as when he had been very young, no one bolted the front door.

Adam turned to Rockford and asked, "Does Father spend a lot of time in the den?"

"Yes, Master Adam. There are several mornings when I find him asleep at his desk. If I can be honest with you, your father talks to himself a lot. There have been many nights when I didn't bolt just the front door, but also my bedroom door. I have done this to keep him from leaving the house.

"One night, before I went to bed, your father had gone to bed earlier than usual. I was picking up the living room when I saw him walk through the front door, talking in his sleep. He was saying, 'You are home again, Amy. Peter didn't help you. I did.' After this happened, I couldn't go to sleep unless I bolted my bedroom door as well. I don't understand why your father is doing this now."

"Thank you for telling me all of this. I will do what it takes to fix this." Adam turned toward the door and kept walking.

When Rockford shut the door, Adam could hear the deadbolt latch. Standing against the outside of the door, he said, "Who's Peter?"

24

Struggles and Accountability

The next morning at work was pretty much the same thing that went on every day since I started working there. As soon as I arrived, Doctor Phillips handed me a stack of papers to enter into his office computer. Even though the numbers were different, it was basically the same thing. I waited on getting copies as today he didn't leave.

Soon, Doctor Belmar entered the office room. "How are you, Malon?" he asked.

"Good, and thanks for asking," I said, still trying to make all of them believe that I loved my job and wouldn't do anything to jeopardize losing it, so that maybe they could stop suspecting me.

Doctor Belmar walked to Doctor Phillips' office door, knocked once, and opened the door, making sure that the door was shut tightly behind him.

"Terry, I have been expecting you. I spoke with Ann last night. Everything on her end is going very well. Today I checked the electromagnetic energy readings again. The energy coming from Sleeping Indian Mountain is registering strong on my meter and lab computer. The feedback from the condensation and water vapor are too high. It is drawing a lot of publicity from the townspeople and the news reports from Applegrove. Before we leave the area to come back here, we have no choice but to adjust it. This will need to also be monitored before we can claim bragging rights."

"Everything that will stay there, Shawn, when we leave, will be worth bragging about," Doctor Belmar replied with a wild, wide-eyed, psychotic stare with his crazy eyes focused on Doctor Phillips.

"What do you mean by everything that stays behind, Terry?"

"Everything that isn't important to me. I have a promise to keep and I'm keeping it!"

"I need to do more monitoring Terry. On your way out, tell Malon that she can leave early again today. Also, I need to talk with Ann again."

"I will show myself out after I tell Malon and Ann what you requested."

At that moment, Doctor Phillips was feeling uncomfortable. Words that came from Doctor Belmar's mouth, the look on his face and in his eyes were not those of a successful scientist.

Before leaving, I was told that Doctor Phillips had given him the report for me to go home for the day. I had just enough time when the two doctors were talking, to get copies of the papers I was given to put in the computer.

Doctor Belmar had occupied Doctor Phillips for just the right amount of time. I was quick to grab what I needed and leave my office room. Another early day. Wrapping all of this up couldn't come soon enough for me.

What I didn't know was that after I left, Doctor Belmar had gone to his lab to take his turn at monitoring and measuring the specimen's activity. Doctor Neil gave her report to him, expecting to leave the building right away. Before going, Doctor Belmar told her that Doctor Phillips needed to speak with her. When she saw that I had left for the day, she knocked on his office door, entered, and Doctor Neil made sure the office door was securely shut.

"What is so important, Shawn? I am ready to leave right now."

"Ann, I am glad this project is going well, but I am a little concerned about Terry. He has been pushing himself on this project to what I believe is the breaking point. Have you looked at his eyes lately? When I was speaking with him earlier, he was staring at me with wild, crazy, glazed open eyes. He hasn't cared about playing golf in weeks. He is obsessed to finish this in record time. Actually, I feel that he wants to fix what's bad way too soon. I'm not convinced that everything here is what it should be. I have my doubts for all of our safety. I know he won't give it another week of testing, which is really what should happen. He made a comment earlier that concerns me. He said he was leaving behind on the mountain what didn't matter to him. I think even you, Ann, know what he is referring to and bringing back."

"Yes, Shawn, I have noticed a bigger change in Terry. We have the option to get out of this research project right now and go back to Switzerland. Personally, I would like to see it completed, as we have worked very hard alongside Terry for twenty years. I, too, have seen his eyes change as well."

"You are right, Ann. We have been working hard to see this project completed and to be recognized for what it is, but neither one of us can afford to be connected to Terry and his father's screw-up. They created this horror, and we are in the middle of it.

"After I take my turn tomorrow at monitoring, I will let you know my decision. I might not be going with you and Terry to Applegrove. My credibility and life come first. I am convinced that Terry is pushing this research too fast. I think he might be going insane. He has changed, Ann!"

"I agree with you on the monitoring. Before we both make a decision, let's give it more thought. Terry might be somewhat insane right now. I think he is insane with power. He is, and has been, recognized as the best scientist in his field of research.

"We come in second, Shawn. If we didn't believe in what we have been researching for the past twenty years, we wouldn't be here now. Just keep in mind that if this does work, we will be credited with discovering what will change the world. I want to believe in our research and that what you see in Terry's eyes is him wanting his research to turn out right this time. He already knows that he needs to undo what his father and himself messed up."

"Okay. We will keep working on this for now."

All of that being said, Doctor Neil left to go home. Adam and Rockford weren't the only ones who had noticed the change in Doctor Terry Belmar. It appeared that Doctor Phillips was starting to rethink the final outcome of their research, whereas Doctor Neil might just want recognition. Twenty years is a long time, and maybe a part of her heart had developed feelings for Doctor Belmar.

Back in Applegrove, my father had gone to town, to once again convince the townspeople that help would be coming soon, and to stay put in their homes and stay off the mountain because the man who created the terror that had taken away their way of life for many years would be there soon to stop it.

This news worked for some, but Sam had lost his wife and was out for blood and revenge. He wanted to make Doctor Belmar pay. He wanted to kill him himself! Who could blame him for feeling the way he did? No one in the town did.

They finally agreed that in a few more days, no matter whether Doctor Belmar was there or not, they were going to start walking up Sleeping Indian Mountain with all the rifles and handguns that they could find. No man would be coming down off the mountain until whatever these people were had been destroyed.

At the time, they didn't know that it would take more than weapons to make the mountain, and all the surrounding towns, normal and safe again.

This would come later.

While Doctor Neil was at her home, Doctor Phillips was working and Doctor Belmar was in his lab, writing down the electro waves from the electrical charge that was registering on his meter and computer. The activity kept increasing. All the readings gave Doctor Belmar assurance that his research was a success. At least he *believed* it was.

At my hotel room, Adam had returned. He had the copies. After checking them and comparing them to the copies he had looked at the night before, he said, "Mylo, I am convinced that this is from an electromagnetic force or field somewhere. I saw Father last night. He told me that he wouldn't be at his house tonight and would be working on his research. Rockford, his butler, is dead-bolting the front door at night now after Father goes to bed. He has been sleepwalking and coming back through the front door, talking to my mother.

"When I got there, I walked into his den and saw him sitting at his desk, talking to an old photo of Mother, telling her that he would make it right this time, and that a man by the name of Peter didn't do what he promised Father and Grandfather he would do. He said that this man got scared and left. I didn't have a chance to ask him any of what I overheard him saying, as his pager sounded and he left the den to go call Ann. When he did come back to the den, he announced that he needed to go to bed. I keep wondering who Peter is. He might have the answers we need."

"Adam, remember when I came back from Applegrove? I told you about all the stories that were shared with me. One of the stories came from a man by the name of Ralph Winters. He told me about the traveling salesman that had gone to a man's house that lived just below Sleeping Indian Mountain. This man's name was Peter Barnes. Ralph Winters said everyone in town believed he was a scientist that practiced black magic. Do you think maybe that might be who your father is talking about?"

"It might be. After I leave here tonight, I want you to call your father and ask him if he will go to Peter Barnes' house to either speak to him or gather important information. According to Father, he left the area, but he still might be hiding out in his house."

"I will call right away. Soon with answers, all of this will be a thing of the past."

What I told Adam was a true fact, but no one could change all the damage that had been done already to the people who lived in Applegrove either their entire life or most of their lives. The struggles that they went through to make a good life for themselves and their families, just to see it all destroyed by a couple of scientists from New York City, that in their sick minds, thought they could change the world. No matter what Doctor Belmar, Doctor Phillips and Doctor Neil did now to try to undo what had been done many years ago, they would be held accountable for everything!

25

Traveling and Surviving

As soon as Adam left for the night, I called my father, who explained to me what was said in Applegrove at the country store. I then asked him for help requested by Adam.

"Father, Adam needs you to go to Peter Barnes' house, and if he is there, maybe you can get him to talk. If he doesn't, then maybe you can gather some more information from the house. The other night, Doctor Belmar was talking to a photo of Adam's mother, and was overheard by Adam muttering the name Peter. We are not sure that the Peter who lives below the mountain is the same Peter that Doctor Belmar was talking about, but things are adding up to look that way."

"I can do this, Mylo, but as far as I know, Peter Barnes skipped town. In his old house there might be some things that might be of importance. I will go first thing tomorrow morning to check it all out."

"Be careful, Father. You heard the story from Ralph Winters on what the traveling salesman told him."

"I will, and you be careful, as from what I just

heard, it sounds like Adam's father is totally insane. He is capable of anything."

"Don't worry, Father, I am very much aware of just what all three of the doctors are about, and capable of."

The next day I made it to work on time with the same papers waiting for me on my desk. No sign of Doctor Phillips. I checked the hallway, to see if I could tell if anyone was coming. Today was the third day for me to copy the daily report for Adam.

After several hours of being done with what I needed to do, I was getting impatient. I wanted to open the old file cabinet and look for more secret compartments. Out of fear, I chose not to. Something, or some*one*, kept telling me not to. Also, I kept wondering if Adam was able to hack into Doctor Phillips' office computer. If he could, he might be able to get more information than I could find in the old file cabinet.

I had poured a cup of coffee, trying to relax at my desk, when Doctor Belmar walked through my office room door. For once in my life, it was a good thing that I listened to my inner self.

"Malon, I just came by to tell you that Doctor Phillips is going to be in the lab all day today. He asked me to stop in here and tell you to go ahead and leave now."

"Thank you, Doctor Belmar. I will do just that."

When he left the office room, I thought that it might be safe, but just took the copies from my desk, folded them this time, and put them under my jacket before I, too, walked out of my office room.

I was so glad I did, because when I stepped outside the office door, I was met by Doctor Neil. She asked me if I had seen Doctor Belmar. I told her yes, and that she had just missed him. She assured me that in the next day or two, plans were for them to leave the city for a while and that if they did leave, I would be working for Adam, alongside his office assistant, Diane.

She didn't know, nor would she know, that when the three doctors left for Applegrove, Adam and I wouldn't be far behind them.

At my hotel room, my thoughts were on my father. I knew he would go there alone and not involve anyone else in his venture.

In Applegrove, Father had made his way through the bad fog and low clouds to Peter Barnes' house. Because of the low, thick clouds, Father could barely see to walk to the front door of the old house. If there was anything or anyone around, or beside him, it would be too late to run to his truck or to the house. The front door of the old house was a ways from where he had parked.

He was afraid, but determined to do as Adam and I requested him to do. The thought of all the men making the trip up the mountain in a few days—walking instead of driving—made him feel fearful for everyone.

When he reached the front door, out of respect, he knocked and called out Peter's name. No noise came from inside of the house. No one had seen

Peter nor his wife for many years. There were rumors around town of how Peter and his wife might have been killed and eaten. Or how the walking people might have scared them out of their house, and to a different town, or city. Nobody knew for sure.

Whatever the reason was, why he wasn't there, his front door was unlocked. Father called out to Peter and no one answered. Father felt strange going into another man's house without permission or his being there. He had come there for information and would look through whatever he could find. He had called Peter's name many times with no answer, so Father entered the house.

He went up the stairs, calling Peter's name. He looked in every room and found no one. When he went downstairs, he looked through cupboards and drawers. He found nothing of importance to help us. Father made his way up the stairs again, where he proceeded to look through everything there. As Father looked around a bedroom, he saw a fold-down old desk. There was no way he could open it. He looked for a hidden key. He even checked through dresser drawers and the closet, to see if maybe Peter had secretly put it in there.

The one thing that had never let him down in his life was an old pocketknife that he carried with him all the time. Using the tip of the knife, he was able to turn the old lock. He raised the top of the desk and rolled it back. Father felt, at that moment, like he had found a gold mine. In the old desk was a book that gave him chills. The book had many pages of what appeared to be research and rituals of black magic. The pages that weren't about black magic or voodoo had numbers that Peter could have used in measuring something. The ritualistic practices of black magic and voodoo more than likely were used by Peter, the scientist practicing both.

All of this together would give Adam the information that he was after. Father heard a sound coming from downstairs. Now was the time for him to leave the house ... *and fast!* He waited for a few minutes, hiding in a closet to listen. He couldn't leave the bedroom at that time, if whatever was down there was coming up the stairs.

When he didn't hear any noise of footsteps coming up the stairs, he quietly walked to the bedroom door, opened it carefully, and looked both ways. He left the room, walking softly down each stair.

After the last step, he ran to the front door, opened it, and ran in the direction of his truck. After entering it, he locked all doors, started it, and sped away, not looking back. Father was a strong man who didn't fear explainable things, but the unknown awakening was making him more afraid than he had ever been in his life. What he had found that day should be enough information for Adam.

When Father returned home, he called me to tell me what had taken place, and what he had from the old fold-down desk. I assured him that what he had would be of tremendous help. Later that day,

Adam would call him.

Whereas in the lab, Doctor Phillips with his meter, and Doctor Belmar's lab computer were hitting and seeing higher levels of activity. This project had worked, but the question still bothering Doctor Phillips was how *well* did it work?

Adam had called his father and was told that Doctor Phillips, Doctor Neil and himself were leaving the city sometime tomorrow morning. He wanted Adam to report while they were away. Having the heads-up that we needed, he and I would be packed and waiting to leave at the exact moment all three doctors walked out of the Wayne Belmar Research Industries building door.

A surprise for Doctor Belmar and the other two doctors would be there on Sleeping Indian Mountain, about the same time they arrived. There would be no more secrets!

I heard a knock. Adam was with me again. He explained the plan he had for us. I told him that tomorrow I would be packed and ready to leave when he came to take me to the office. Adam was ready to speak with my father. Never in my life did I think that this would be, under these circumstances, the first phone call meeting of my father and the man that I had fallen in love with.

"Mr. Moore, it's Adam Belmar."

"Adam, it's good to finally talk to you on the phone."

"Yes, it is, sir. Mylo said you found out something today that is important."

"When I went to Peter Barnes' house, he wasn't there. I searched the house and found several papers with numbers. Also pages of black magic and voodoo that were in a book that looked like rituals. I got spooked as I did hear a noise downstairs. I left, hoping that what I found will help you."

"It has. Thank you for doing this for me. I will be in contact with you in a few days, unless plans change. As of now, my father and the other two doctors will be on their way to Sleeping Indian Mountain tomorrow. I wish I knew the right words to express to all of you how sorry I am for what my father and Grandfather created in your area, and on the mountain. I know all of you have lost a lot because of it."

"Thank you, Adam. Please just take good care of our girl."

"Don't worry, I won't let anyone or anything hurt her. I give you my word," Adam told Father as he squeezed and rubbed my hand.

"I believe you, Adam. We will talk in a couple of days."

Their conversation ended. Now it was time for Adam and I to talk.

"Mylo, today I was able to hack into Shawn's office computer. I was right. He has been measuring electromagnetic energy from a force field. My guess is that it is coming from either Applegrove or Sleeping Indian. Also, I found out the combination to my father's lab. Tomorrow morning, before we leave—providing everything is still going good and I have time—I am going in there to see what all of them have been working on.

"When we see my father on Sleeping Indian Mountain and I catch him, Shawn and Ann in the act of what they will be doing up there, at that time I will confront all three of them face to face.

"Your father told me that he found papers with numbers and a book with black magic or voodoo rituals in it. I think the papers are like the ones we have here. I am starting to believe the townspeople in Applegrove. It sounds like Peter Barnes might have been trying to raise the dead.

"Then again, it isn't *possible*. There is more to it than that. The dead can't jump out of their resting places. None of this makes any sense to me at all!"

"I agree with you. This is so bizarre. I guess right now, until we know the truth about the secrets of Sleeping Indian, we have no choice but to continue with our plan. We can choose what we want to believe. Sometimes reality is fiction, and then again, fiction is reality."

What we had talked about was a deep subject. Was it possible that Peter, Doctor Terry Belmar and Doctor Wayne Belmar were able to make dead men walk again, or was there actually more to this? There had to be, because of the research the last twenty years.

Adam left, and I was packing a bag for our journey to Applegrove. Father and Mother didn't know I was coming home to Sleeping Indian, and it was best to keep it that way. When things were taken care of, they would see me—and meet Adam.

26

Facing Trouble

Early in the morning I was wide awake. I was excited about going home, but fearful of what I would witness on Sleeping Indian Mountain.

A knock on the door told me that Adam was here to pick me up for work. Today would be the last day I would be working at Wayne Belmar Research Industries building.

When he walked me to my office, we were met by Doctor Belmar and Doctor Neil.

"Adam, my boy, Ann and I came by here to let you know that we are going to go eat at the cafeteria, and then all three of us will be on our way out of the city. Malon is working for you right now. Shawn is supposed to meet us in an hour in the parking lot. He went back to my lab to get a few things. When he comes out, tell him to take the specimen to the trailer. We are taking it with us."

"As you wish, Father. I will see you very soon."

Doctor Belmar had no idea what he was in for when his eyes looked into Adam's on Sleeping Indian Mountain.

They walked away, and Adam and I went into my office room. We were waiting for Doctor Phillips to return and knew we had one hour before he needed to meet with Doctor Belmar and Doctor Neil. It was starting to look as if Adam wouldn't get the chance to go into his father's lab.

Within thirty minutes Doctor Phillips returned. Adam gave him the instructions to bring the specimen with him. After a lot of mumbling and complaining about how he should get even with Adam's father and Doctor Neil, as he had stuff in his office to bring as well, he stormed out, saying, "Now I need to be the only one to get the specimen?"

Adam knew that there was an elevator that also was private that went from his father's lab to the underground parking lot, where the trailer was sitting. There was a good chance that he wouldn't find anything in there of much use to us after Doctor Phillips left.

A few minutes before the departure time, Adam decided it was too late to check the lab. We would be leaving the city with what knowledge we already had. We took a side door, and an elevator to Adam's car. We scrunched down in the seat and watched, and waited as Doctor Phillips slid a gurney into the trailer. Whatever the specimen was, it wasn't small.

Soon Doctor Belmar and Doctor Neil came out of an elevator. As they walked to the trailer, Doctor Phillips had made himself more upset with the other two doctors for giving him so much to do, with no help from either one of them. He informed them that because they had made him do most of the work, he was off duty until they reached Sleeping Indian. These were words that he would regret later.

Doctor Belmar locked the trailer door and climbed into his Suburban. Soon after, they left the spot they were parked in. Adam gave them a few minutes to get out of the parking lot and then we were on our journey behind them.

Not knowing that my father had left a message on my hotel phone answering machine, he had said, "Mylo, it's your father. We had a town meeting again, and even with all the information I had to share with everyone, I was outnumbered in votes. Things are getting worse here every day, and I can't hold anyone back. There will be fifty-one of us going up the mountain tomorrow by foot. Don't worry, as we are going to be loaded with different weapons to protect ourselves. We are going to put an end to this nonsense once and for all. I will talk to you and Adam in a few days. Hopefully, his father gets here soon, and can make this go away. Your mother will be fine and safe. Don't worry about me. I love you, Mylo."

This was a message that I wouldn't ever hear. If I had received it in time for me to take a plane to Applegrove, instead of riding with Adam in his car, I probably would have taken the plane. Father would have protested my walking up the mountain with him and the others, but I would have been there with a rifle in my hands to protect myself and my father. He wasn't a young man anymore.

I thought that after the other men in the town

had heard everything that was up to date, they would stay and wait for the arrival of the three doctors.

Adam and I were far enough behind the trailer that none of them could see us. When we reached the top of Sleeping Indian Mountain, we wouldn't be kept in the shadows anymore. The truth would be known.

Several hours of driving had passed. Doctor Belmar drove into a motel. They were stopped for the night. To our advantage, there was a motel across from theirs. We were able to get rooms and found a place close by where we could eat. Adam knew his father would stay in his motel room and order in for all three of them. This was always his father's and mother's tradition that they'd enjoyed in his younger years of traveling on vacations and road trips.

After eating, we walked around the area, holding hands and looking in store windows. We both knew that our love for one another had grown. The agreement as the night of fun ended for us was to go to bed, and come daylight, sit in the car and watch for the doctors to leave in the morning.

Up at 4:00 A.M. and while waiting for Adam, I called the home phone. The only thing that I said to Mother and Father was, "I love you." The phone rang, but there was no answer, so the words said to them, as well as the message that my father said to me, ended up on an answering machine. I didn't know that they weren't home and that Mother was in our town church with all the other wives and children of the other men who followed my father in his journey walking up the mountain.

Father was at the store with fifty men, waiting for the first sign of daylight. From there, they would leave the old country store in search of a way to make their town and their families safe again. When light came slightly through the clouds, Father said, "Let's go for it." Everyone agreed.

Stuffing food in backpacks alongside their boxes of bullets, they grabbed many weapons and left the store, determined to reach the top of the mountain within a couple of days.

As Adam and I sat in his car, waiting for all three doctors to leave, we talked.

"Adam, with what we have learned, do you have an idea of what the secret could be?"

"I thought about it last night before I went to sleep. I don't believe in dead people walking, but I do know that any form of magic such as black magic and voodoo can be dangerous. Anyone that dabbles in that is asking for trouble. I think the metal boxes that were talked about play a part in this.

"My research was to get the human brains that Father furnished for me to function again. The specimen in the trailer is not small and could be some kind of an animal. Like you, I can't wait to get on the mountain to see the walking creatures and find out what my father has to say about everything, and how he thinks he can make things better as he has done so much damage. I feel that his intentions are for his own gain. He has no regard to his actions that created all this, and he is being selfish, uncaring and—in his heart—has no regrets for what he has done, or is doing now. I am hoping I can stop what he is going to do there, to just use this to gain more fame and fortune."

"I agree, Adam." Even with everything Adam had said, as true as it was, I knew that in Adam's heart he just wanted the father back that he'd had many years ago, who was sane and normal again. As for the damage that his father had caused, there was no way of changing that. This Doctor Belmar would have to pay for, if he even got off the mountain without getting shot himself for what he'd done.

In Applegrove all the men were still climbing up the mountain. As they walked, listening and looking around, they knew that they not only had to protect themselves but also every man who was there. With Father was Ralph Winters, Harry Albert, John Relms, the mayor, Mike Baker, the photographer that went hiking to take pictures but instead had found the metal boxes, my old boss at the country store's husband, Steve, and other ranchers who had lost most of their livestock and everything they owned.

They had a long ways to go on foot. Every branch that snapped under their feet, every bush that rustled from the wind startled them, but they kept walking, listening and watching. There was an old cave that my father knew about. If they made it that far, it would give them shelter and, hopefully, safety for the night.

Nothing had appeared, and the thought on their minds was if these creatures had gone to Applegrove, were their families safe?

The fog was thick and with the low clouds it was hard to see. Before long it was going to rain. They couldn't reach the cave soon enough. All of them were tired, hungry, nervous and afraid.

While we were driving, we saw Doctor Belmar pull over to the side of the highway. We couldn't pass him, so Adam pulled over as well, to watch what they did and why they had stopped. Doctor Belmar, Doctor Phillips and Doctor Neil climbed out of the Suburban and went to the back of the trailer. Adam said he saw a meter in Doctor Phillips' hand that measured activity in the atmosphere, or an electrical charge. Either they had a computer set up in the trailer to measure all of this, or they were doing a daily check on the specimen.

What was this specimen that they were carrying in the back of the trailer? A monster of some sort? After several minutes, they climbed down off the trailer, locked the door and returned to the Suburban. Then all of us were driving toward Applegrove once again.

It was getting late and I was back in eastern Colorado. Tomorrow I would be home.

At the next town, Doctor Belmar stopped again for the night, so that they could all rest. This time Adam and I weren't so lucky as the night before. There was only one motel in this town, and our situation got somewhat sticky. Adam pulled the car over to the curb and waited for Doctor Belmar to go to the motel office to get three rooms for that night. We were far enough away that no one could see us.

After all three doctors were in their rooms, Adam drove into the motel parking lot. I ducked down so that no one could see me and waited for him to return to the car after signing us up for motel rooms as well for the night. When he returned to his car, he said, "Mylo, we need to hurry."

I grabbed his hand and we ran to his motel room. There we would stay. There would be no walking the streets tonight. The drapes were shut, the AC was on, and it was time to call the pizza man.

After a short time, there was a knock on the door. Adam looked through the little peep hole to see who it was. Then someone said, "Pizza guy is here." I giggled and pulled chairs up to the small table in the room. It was time to eat, talk and laugh.

Whereas on the mountain, it had started raining. Father and the other men had found the cave and were there to stay until morning. There was no way to block it off. They would be taking turns all night, watching the opening while others slept.

One thing they noticed was that there was felt by all a slight electrical charge in the air of the cave. No one who had been there before on the mountain had noticed it when they had seen the creatures. Then again, after looking at them and running for their lives, how could they? The only thought on their minds at that time was staying alive!

27

Fear and Loss

Waking up in my home state already felt good to me. In only a matter of hours, we would be driving up the old road leading to the top of Sleeping Indian Mountain. Today was the day.

The routine was the same as yesterday. A slight knock at the motel room door and Adam and I were running to his car. He parked where we could see the back of the trailer, but Doctor Belmar, Doctor Phillips and Doctor Neil wouldn't be able to see us.

It wasn't long until all three doctors were standing at the back of the trailer. Doctor Belmar had unlocked the trailer door and they all climbed in to shut the door behind them. This time they were inside the trailer longer. How Adam and I wished we could hear what they were talking about.

Inside the trailer, Doctor Belmar looked at Doctor Neil and Doctor Phillips and said, "This is amazing. The brain activity is higher than it has ever been. The electrical charge in here is more than we have seen. The electromagnetic force is working, but will need to be toned down when we get there. We will need to be able to see and work when we get on top of the mountain. There will be no stopping until we are standing on Sleeping Indian Mountain."

Doctor Neil and Doctor Phillips agreed. They climbed out of the trailer, locking the door. Soon after, Doctor Belmar backed up as Adam did his car. We were all on our way to the mountain.

On Sleeping Indian, Father and the other men were awake and on their way, climbing up the mountainside. For now, the rain had stopped and the trees and brush were thicker, and the walking would be slower.

No one talked because all the men wanted this to be a surprise attack on the flesh-eating creatures—if one was spotted. Branches snapped, bushes rustled and the wind blew. They kept trudging upward. When they stopped to rest, one of the men said, "Where's Howard?"

"I don't know. He was with us when we went into the cave last night. We were all so jammed in there, I didn't think to do a head count this morning," Father replied.

Ralph Winters spoke up and said, "I took the last shift of watching the opening. I dozed off a few times. During the early morning, maybe Howard went outside to smoke."

"Did anyone see him this morning?" Father asked. "I didn't."

Every man there said no. They weren't sure if Howard had gotten scared and left to go back down the mountain, or if he had wandered off and was attacked.

What they didn't know was that before daylight, when everyone was asleep, Howard woke up in a cold sweat. His anxiety was out of control and he felt penned in with everyone there. He was a coal miner and had survived a cave-in at the coal mine where he worked. He still had flashbacks from being trapped for hours, so Howard grabbed his backpack and gun. He was running down the mountain to go home when he tripped from a hole he couldn't see. He hit the ground and was too far away for anyone to hear his screams for help. His foot was broken. Out of the bushes and trees, the creatures emerged and found him.

Howard yelled and cried out in pain as his flesh was torn away from his neck and torso. They had jerked his arms and legs off. After the creatures feasted on his whole body, they stumbled away.

Not knowing for sure where Howard was, or the direction in which he went, the men decided to keep going. Father swallowed hard as he was pretty sure that there was no hope for Howard now. More than likely, he was dead, and finding his body would need to wait until their trip down the mountainside.

We were getting closer. Doctor Belmar was driving faster. His intent was to be there before dark. What I didn't understand was the fact that he had to know how dangerous the people that walked were, and yet he wasn't afraid. What did he have in the back of that trailer besides his specimen and the mini lab?

The clouds were becoming heavier and lower, as well as the fog. This was making it harder to watch for invaders as Father and the others kept walking. Their feet were sore and swollen. Their arms and backs were tired from carrying the rifles and handguns. It was a long journey up to the top of the mountain.

We passed the small town where I had arrived by plane. Everything was going as planned.

John Relms spotted something in the trees and fog. It was too far away for him to see what it was. Every man there was nervous and skittish, but they were ready to fight and kill whatever it was. They took a rest and waited for the things to come closer. Their rifles were fully loaded.

Doctor Belmar had reached the turnoff and was on the old road, headed up the mountain, driving very slowly.

It was the middle of the day, but because of all the fog and low cloud coverage, it looked like evening. In spite of the terrific fog and low clouds, Adam was able to stay closer enough behind his father without using his headlights. We were waiting for Doctor Belmar to reach the top of the mountain. Then, after watching briefly, we would join the three doctors on top of Sleeping Indian Mountain.

In the Suburban, Doctor Belmar talked to

Doctor Phillips and Doctor Neil. "We are almost there," he said. "The fog and clouds are worse than I expected. When we first get there, we have work to do. I still remember where they are at. We have no choice but to tone this down."

Within about ten minutes as we followed far enough back as not to be seen, but close enough to know what they were doing, Doctor Belmar reached the top of the mountain. We sat in Adam's car, watching to see what they did first. Soon we would join them.

A ways away, Father and the other men were almost to the top when, out of nowhere, they were met by several pale, grotesque, walking people stumbling toward all of them. These things had dried blood on their clothes and faces. They were hungry again and looking to make another kill for their feast.

Father yelled out for them to stop, not knowing if for some weird, unknown way, these things could understand him. He had to try to communicate with them, if possible. Without any success, the creatures kept stumbling and making their way down the mountainside. They could smell living flesh and it was time for them to eat again.

The mayor, John Relms, told everyone that they couldn't afford to waste bullets, so they should let them get closer and then fire their rifles. That would have worked, except there were more of the creatures that were behind some of the men. As these men were checking their rifles and concentrating on the ones stumbling down the mountain toward them, they didn't hear those that had reached them from behind.

With guns raised and ready to fire, the men in the front heard horrific screams behind them. The creatures were on top of four of the men in the rear. Father turned and fired at these flesh-eating monsters, but it was too late to save his friends. They had already torn the necks out of these men as they lay there, dying. Beside them were the creatures that Father had shot and killed. The creatures coming at them from the front were stumbling and bumping into each other as they got closer.

John Relms yelled out, *"Fire!"*

Forty-six of the remaining men still living lifted their rifles and started shooting. Father had killed four of the unknown monsters behind them and he and the others left killed ten that were in front of them. Not sure if more were in the trees, waiting to attack them, the men kept walking up the mountainside.

As Adam and I sat, waiting to approach his father, I heard the gunfire on the mountain. I knew then that this had to be coming from my father and the other men with him. I knew they were facing trouble and were in danger.

I began to panic. I told Adam that I was sure my father and the other men were close by and that we needed to do something!

"Mylo, I, too, heard the shots. We have waited

long enough for me to see what they are doing. Now I am going to confront my father!"

Adam drove his car to the top of the mountain and we got out. The three doctors had heard the car coming toward them and also the shots that were being fired. As we walked closer, Doctor Belmar also was walking toward us. The look on his face told us that he was not happy to see us.

It was question-and-answer time and Doctor Belmar knew it!

28

No Way to Change What Is

When Doctor Belmar was standing beside us, he yelled at Adam and said, "Adam, what are you doing here? You know better than to follow me! I told you to stay in New York City and work on the research I expected you to complete before I got back!"

"Father, I really don't care what you expected me to do! I have gone through years of my life knowing that you and Grandfather had kept a secret from me. If not for Malon coming to the city, I would never have realized that everything you told me was a lie, and that there was more to the research now that you, Shawn and Ann have been doing for twenty years of not just your life, but mine as well! I am tired of secrets and lies! With research of our own, we have discovered many things that you have been doing. How dare you risk, kill and destroy other people's lives like you have!"

"Adam, I am sorry that you have found out so much. Shawn and Ann tried to warn me about Malon, but I wouldn't listen. She had no right snooping into our business and trying to destroy the relationship that you and I have, as father and son!"

"Father, I am thankful for Malon. We have grown very close, and it isn't her fault that you and Grandfather created something that is horrific to others. You can't blame her for what you did, and I will not let you stand here and do it!"

"I don't care about the people here in this area, Adam. Many years ago, Grandfather and I did something to try to help. If the people here in this small redneck area got hurt, it isn't my problem, and you shouldn't have made it yours!"

Not sure what Doctor Belmar meant by that last remark, or what he and the other doctors were going to do next, I felt fearful. Were they so determined to go down in history as being the great scientists that changed the world, that they would do anything to keep their secret, or could Adam make his father tell him everything?

"Father, you, Grandfather, Shawn and Ann should be ashamed of yourselves. There is no way to change the world doing what I believe you have done ... and are about to do! I remember before Mother got killed, the kind, generous man and father you were. All I see now is a lonely glory seeker that wants fame and fortune, and will stop at nothing to get it! I am tired of you keeping all the secrets of Sleeping Indian Mountain all these years. This started twenty years ago, and then you brought Shawn and Ann into your sick and twisted world that you have been living since Mother passed away. I won't let you continue to destroy people any longer, like you have done! I want the truth, and I want it now!"

By then, Doctor Belmar's eyes had changed again to the wild, open-eyed, staring look that Adam had seen before. He was ready to talk, and this time I believed that he would tell Adam everything we had been waiting to hear.

"Adam, when your mother was killed, I couldn't stand the thought of never seeing her again. I tried so hard to accept her death, but was sinking in a pool of depression. Your grandfather came up with an idea. I listened. Grandfather believed that your Uncle Peter could help. He had moved back here. This was the place where your mother had come to when she was very young. She used to spend summers here and wanted to live in Applegrove.

"Instead, she met me in the city, where your grandfather had started his research business that you have known your whole life. Your Uncle Peter was also Grandfather's son from another woman. I didn't tell you about him because Grandfather hardly saw him. Twenty years ago, Peter turned to black magic and voodoo. He also was a great scientist that did research on it and believed that he could use it to his advantage. Grandfather was researching the aspects of cloning at that time. He told me that with your mother's DNA, he could create a woman just like her. I knew it would take many years to complete this research, and I was afraid I would be too old, or that the probability of it working wouldn't happen.

"In the city, Grandfather and I decided to put it

all together into one research project. We used the cloning DNA, parts from other people that had passed away, and the black magic from Uncle Peter. So with all of this knowledge and reconstruction, as your mother was kept on ice, we also brought other bodies with us in the trailer. We took them from a mortuary in the city and paid the owner money to look the other way. With the bodies on ice, we managed to keep a lot of the organs working that didn't stop functioning. We put blood back into your mother and replaced the brain that had been destroyed. We even dug up graves here at the cemetery. We transferred parts to those bodies that were recently buried.

"We actually thought that this would work as it should have. Then we installed metal boxes that we had researched and put together in my lab. Inside them we created water vapor and other parts to create an electromagnetic force field. The water vapor made fog, which combined, made droplets that stayed in the air. This vapor turned to a gas and was invisible. The low clouds were made from the water vapor as well. The air changed into liquid water and the low clouds became condensation, which caused the ground level fog that continues to become thicker.

"All of this, Adam, as a scientist, is nothing that you already don't know about. We needed the fog and the clouds to form so that we could do our work and research here without being seen by any-one who might come up here. Before we left, Grandfather was supposed to check it, to make sure

that it was where it should be and that all the metal
boxes were working properly. He didn't have it right.
We made sure that we could monitor all of this in
the city.

"After our hard work of administering blood
back in the bodies and repairing their organs and
other parts of so many bodies that we watched for
days, even though Grandfather was very leery of
Peter and his black magic and voodoo, we trusted
him anyway. Grandfather said that with the cloning
in the test tubes and the parts that we had taken off
of other bodies and put in unknown graves, and with
Peter's help in raising these people up, that there
would be many families who would get back the
people they'd lost because of death.

"Grandfather and I continued to monitor everything here—with everything in the universe being
made out of energy, and our consciousness influenced
by it with behavior to restructure it. The metal
boxes not only created fog and clouds, it also gave
energy to the bodies. With all the rituals from the
black magic and voodoo, things started to look like it
would work. Even with the cloning that we did, that
was supposed to work as well. After Grandfather
and I left here, the bodies did start walking and they
were feeding on animals on the mountain.

"Then things went wrong when they tasted
human flesh. Animals had been working for them,
but they wanted human flesh as well. The brains
you reconstructed were supposed to help them to
walk right, talk and be able to go back to their

homes before they passed away. This trip was to trap them all in one place so that we could put them to sleep and replace the brains they now have with reconstructed ones that you worked on in your lab. After twenty years of research, Adam, we have it right. Every meter reading that we have done is checking out good.

"Help us, and you will get credit like us for our creation. Your Uncle Peter couldn't help your mother and the others. After the people started walking and he could see that there were flaws in the research and the black magic and voodoo hadn't completely helped everyone here to be normal again, he got scared and feared for his life, so he left the area. His wife was very strange, and Grandfather believed that he had used his black magic on her as well."

"Father, you know that I cannot take part in any of this. You should have known that you couldn't bring Mother back to the way she was before. There is nothing you can do now but face the fact that you did wrong, and take responsibility for it," Adam replied to his father.

By the time Doctor Belmar and Adam had finished talking, the fog and clouds that hovered over the top of Sleeping Indian Mountain had completely lifted. I could see Father and several men coming through the trees and brush.

Doctor Phillips had gone to the back of the trailer to get the specimen to show Adam that their research was a success and how famous they would be. When he climbed into the back of the trailer, he shut the door behind him. The body of the specimen, because of all the energy and activity in the air, had opened her eyes.

She sat up with Doctor Phillips' back facing her and pulled the sheet down that was covering her whole body. She climbed down and grabbed Doctor Phillips. She was strong and there was no way he could pull himself away from her. She sunk her teeth firmly into his neck and pulled the flesh completely away from the bones.

With torn flesh and a throat that was ripped out, Doctor Phillips' cries for help were senseless. No one could hear him, as he was dead. The creature was trapped inside as she ate her fill from the delusional scientist's body.

I could see Father and the other men coming toward us. They had seen us standing there. Through a small clearing on top of the mountain, we could see what looked to be a hundred walking bodies stumbling toward us.

Doctor Belmar's eyes were still crazy and his insanity had consumed him. These things that the salesman had called the walking dead were ugly, pale, grotesque, repulsive, and they started out in life as normal human beings, but were turned into monster creatures that had no way of knowing who they were in life, and not even knowing that they were dead. This not only was ludicrous, outlandish and bizarre, it was cruel, horrific and something that no one would ever expect to see—ever.

There were three creatures stumbling toward

us when Doctor Belmar yelled out to one of them. "Amy! I knew you would come back to me!"

Adam tried grabbing his father, but failed. Doctor Belmar started running with his arms stretched out toward the walking body of his dead wife. Adam yelled out to his father as loud as he could, "STOP, Father! Come back! That walking body is *not* the woman she was. COME BACK!" he screamed.

Doctor Belmar was completely insane by then. He wanted nothing more than to be with his wife, Amy. He yelled back at Adam, "*No,* Adam! I want to hug your mother. She has come back to us!"

When Doctor Belmar did reach Amy Belmar, who was nothing more than a walking body with a brain that didn't remember anything about her husband, Adam or their life together, she grabbed him. And like the specimen in the back of the trailer, she sunk her teeth into his neck to tear away the flesh and bones. When the other creatures reached him, as they were tearing his arms and legs off to feast on his body, Doctor Belmar was so insane, he was laughing.

Instead of screaming in pain, he just said, "We will be together forever, Amy!" Blood was everywhere. Doctor Belmar was dead.

Adam stood there, watching and crying. He hated it that his last conversation with his father had to be the way it was. His father had been sick for many years and now Doctor Terry Belmar was right where he wanted to be.

As Doctor Neil watched, she was screaming and shaking. She was talking to herself, and then she would scream again. She, too, was going crazy.

When the monsters finished their feast on Doctor Belmar's body, they started stumbling toward the others who were making their way toward us. Doctor Neil was still screaming, and then laughing. She kept saying, "Where is Terry and Shawn?"

As the creatures got closer, Father also was closer to us. He yelled, "Hit the ground!" He had thrown a grenade.

We grabbed Doctor Neil and took her to the ground with us. As it exploded, pieces of the walking bodies flew. Father had destroyed all of them.

Ralph Winters, Harry Albert, John Relms and Mike Baker walked to the back of the trailer. When they swung the door open, they started firing their rifles until they had pumped many rounds into the walking body that had killed and eaten Doctor Phillips.

I ran back to the inside of the Suburban and used Doctor Belmar's car phone to call the country store and the church, to tell Mother to alert the National Guard that the fog and clouds were gone and they were needed on the mountain as soon as they could get there.

It wasn't but a short time later that helicopters landed. Many men jumped down with rifles to secure the area and dispose of all the dead bodies.

Adam ran to what was left of his father's body,

telling the Guardsmen to leave his father there. He would handle the arrangements for him at the mortuary. Adam would bury his father next to the plot of his mother in the old cemetery. Adam had found his mother's arm that still had her wedding ring on the finger. She had lost her life because she wanted to keep her wedding ring. Her arm would be placed back in her casket in her grave, where her entire body should have stayed all along.

Adam came back to me and was met by my father, who hung onto him and heard his cries. It wasn't long and the old school bus drove up the old road leading to the top of the mountain. When it arrived, there were forty-five tired men who climbed on that bus that day. The other five that weren't going home would be retrieved by the National Guard and taken to the morgue like Doctor Belmar and Doctor Phillips.

As for what happened to Doctor Neil, we didn't know except as two Guardsmen were escorting her to the helicopter, she was laughing and asked again, "Where is Terry and Shawn?" More than likely, she was taken to a mental hospital. The secrets of Sleeping Indian Mountain, with all the stories, would be told for many years to come.

Some people will choose to believe that the stories told were meant to give them a perspective of reality with intent of being fiction. All the secrets of the mountain were now laid to rest.

After the mortuary car came and took Doctor Belmar and Doctor Phillips away, the Guardsmen took the specimen out of the back of the trailer. Adam drove his father's Suburban down off of Sleeping Indian, and I drove Adam's car with my father sitting safely beside me.

On our way down the mountain, I told Father the words and explanation of how the creatures came about, and why.

For the first time in years, the sky was blue. The fog was gone and not a cloud was in the sky. We were told that everything would be removed from Sleeping Indian Mountain. This included all the bodies and metal boxes.

Adam and Father had connected. The small town of Applegrove and the surrounding towns were back to normal again.

The next day, Adam buried Doctor Belmar alongside his beloved wife, Amy. A tombstone was placed at his plot with the date of birth, date of death, the name Doctor Terry Belmar, and the words inscribed that said: *"One of the most brilliant scientists in the world."* Adam threw the first shovelful of dirt in the hole on top of his father's casket. The only ones that attended the burial were Adam, Father, Mother and myself.

A tear dropped from Adam's eye. He felt a loss, but also felt peace finally, for his father. What started out with his father wanting to bring his wife back to him and Adam, and to give other families back the persons whom they had lost through death, turned into bodies that killed and destroyed lives of many people, instead of saving them.

Knowing the secrets and that his father was right where he wanted to be—next to his mother—Adam felt peaceful. The words on the tombstone were the truth. Doctor Terry Wayne Belmar was the most brilliant scientist in the world, but even he couldn't change immortality, or the fact that we all are born to live. When our time is up, for whatever reason, we all are supposed to die.

29

Six Years Later

Six years have gone by since the passing of Doctor Belmar and Doctor Phillips. A lot has taken place since then. Three months after their death, my father walked me down the aisle and gave my hand in marriage to Adam.

We thought that with everything that had gone on in Applegrove, Sleeping Indian Mountain and the surrounding towns, the people living there would look down on Adam for what his father and grandfather had started and created twenty years ago. But instead, they welcomed Adam into the community with open arms and attended our wedding. Everyone gave us their blessing.

Since this day, the town and the people in all the areas have prospered. They have restored their land and replenished their livestock and whatever else was lost to them.

After the wedding, Adam and I returned to the city, where he continued to work for the government with research on several projects that were legal and did benefit our world. The old file cabinet was kept, but cleaned out. Everything in there was destroyed. Adam took over his father's office and placed another scientist in his old office, and others in Doctor Phillips' office and Doctor Neil's office.

Doctor Phillips' body was returned to Switzerland and turned over to his family for burial. Adam was told that Doctor Neil still resides in a mental hospital in New York City, where she was taken. That will probably be her home for the rest of her life.

Our first trip back here to Applegrove, I was expecting our son, Josh. The day he was born, Adam and I had gone to Sleeping Indian Mountain to put flowers on all the graves there. As we were coming down the mountain, I went into labor. Mother and Adam were in the delivery room with me when Josh was born. Father was pacing back and forth in the waiting room, anxiously looking at the clock and wearing a path in the carpet until the nurse brought Josh out to meet his grandfather.

This was an emotional day for all of us, especially Adam, who had for many years wondered what the look on his father's face would be, holding his grandchild for the first time.

Even with all the horrible occurrences that led up to that day, Adam and I felt very blessed.

The mayor, John Relms, instructed the county to take down the gate at the bottom of Sleeping Indian Mountain, so that everyone would be allowed on the old road any time of the day or night, to drive to the top of the mountain again. Some of the people in town still felt uncomfortable and questioned going up there, and wondered if everything was taken care of and removed.

The doubt would continue in their minds for many years, if not their entire lives.

Each year, Adam and I return to Applegrove. It has grown some, but is still my beautiful small town. It always will be.

After the birth of Josh, we had a daughter, who was born in the city, to bring back to meet everyone. Her name is Megan. Today is her birthday. She turned 3. Our son, Josh, is 5.

We had a small party for her inside the house tonight. Candles on her cake, ice cream all over her face, and cake in her hair. We all laughed and took pictures to add to our photo album that not only contains ones of Mother, Father, Adam, Josh, Megan and me, but also photos of Adam's mother and father.

With everyone inside the house tonight, I came outside to be alone for a while. I walked to the fence as I had done many times, to look out into the pasture where Rocky once grazed.

I stood there, remembering calmer and more peaceful years. In my mind, I saw myself riding Rocky with Father cheering me on as I raced around the barrels that Father set up for me in the pasture. I remembered, too, the first ride up Sleeping Indian Mountain on Rocky's back when I was Josh's age, with Father holding onto me. With all these memories, I was able to smile.

Standing now at the entrance to the old porch

to the house, all I can hear is the quiet, still, serene night. Many times, as the wind blows, I listen. I believe the wind can and will talk to me in the quietest moments.

If I hadn't lived through and witnessed what I did, I might question the stories of the townspeople. It makes me wonder how the stories will change over many years.

As I stand now inside the back porch, yet again turning out the yard light, I remember it like I was 18 again, saying goodbye to my past and accepting my future. I remember what was said to me just before Adam and I followed Doctor Belmar, Doctor Phillips and Doctor Neil to Sleeping Indian Mountain.

Sometimes a fact is fiction to many people. Then again, is it? Listen to what surrounds you. Don't be afraid ... or should you?